"This is cozy, but you've been avoiding me all weekend."

He nodded.

"We talked about how it would be good to maintain some professional distance," he said. "It didn't seem to work too well, for me anyway. It felt awkward, and I don't want to go through the holiday season that way. So I was thinking we could try being...friends."

"Friends?" She raised an eyebrow.

He nodded. "Friends for the holidays. For us to be friends is best for the children."

"Well..." Her forehead wrinkled. "I guess it's worth a try." She held out a hand, and he shook hers.

He noticed every nuance of her touch. A strong grip. Soft skin, except that he could feel a few calluses. She did a lot of housework and yard work, keeping up this old place.

She seemed to have no reaction to his touch. She just pulled her hand back briskly and smiled.

That was good. This could be managed.

Lee Tobin McClain is the *New York Times* bestselling author of emotional small-town romances featuring flawed characters who find healing through friendship, faith and family. Lee grew up in Ohio and now lives in Western Pennsylvania, where she enjoys hiking with her goofy goldendoodle, visiting writer friends and admiring her daughter's mastery of the latest TikTok dances. Learn more about her books at leetobinmcclain.com.

Books by Lee Tobin McClain

Love Inspired

K-9 Companions

Her Easter Prayer
The Veteran's Holiday Home
A Friend to Trust
A Companion for Christmas
A Companion for His Son
His Christmas Salvation
The Veteran's Valentine Helper
Holding Onto Secrets
Her Surprise Neighbor
An Unexpected Christmas Helper

Rescue Haven

The Secret Christmas Child
Child on His Doorstep
Finding a Christmas Home

Visit the Author Profile page at LoveInspired.com for more titles.

AN UNEXPECTED CHRISTMAS HELPER

LEE TOBIN McCLAIN

If you purchased this book without a cover you should be aware that this book is stolen property. It was reported as "unsold and destroyed" to the publisher, and neither the author nor the publisher has received any payment for this "stripped book."

ISBN-13: 978-1-335-62121-4

Recycling programs for this product may not exist in your area.

An Unexpected Christmas Helper

Copyright © 2025 by Lee Tobin McClain

All rights reserved. No part of this book may be used or reproduced in any manner whatsoever without written permission.

Without limiting the author's and publisher's exclusive rights, any unauthorized use of this publication to train generative artificial intelligence (AI) technologies is expressly prohibited.

This is a work of fiction. Names, characters, places and incidents are either the product of the author's imagination or are used fictitiously. Any resemblance to actual persons, living or dead, businesses, companies, events or locales is entirely coincidental.

For questions and comments about the quality of this book, please contact us at CustomerService@Harlequin.com.

® is a trademark of Harlequin Enterprises ULC.

Love Inspired
22 Adelaide St. West, 41st Floor
Toronto, Ontario M5H 4E3, Canada
www.LoveInspired.com

Printed in Lithuania

Blessed be God, even the Father of our Lord Jesus Christ, the Father of mercies, and the God of all comfort; Who comforteth us in all our tribulation, that we may be able to comfort them which are in any trouble, by the comfort wherewith we ourselves are comforted of God. For as the sufferings of Christ abound in us, so our consolation also aboundeth by Christ.
—*2 Corinthians* 1:3–5

Chapter One

Evan Dukas's shoulders sagged with relief. They'd made it.

He shifted his daughter and the diaper bag to one arm. With his other hand, he knocked on his grandmother's door. "Gramma! I'm here! You home?"

Cold November wind stung his face, and he tried, unsuccessfully, to tighten the hood of the baby's jacket. He could see the kitchen light on. And was that a whiff of Gramma's potato soup? He knocked again.

Lily twisted in his arm, her little face screwing up in an expression he'd already learned meant she was about to cry. He bounced her like he'd seen other parents do, but she clenched her tiny fists and opened her mouth, wide.

He braced himself in anticipation of the noise. In the three days he'd had Lily, he'd learned that she had the lung power of a world-class athlete.

Gramma would know what to do. At ninety, she couldn't be expected to care for Lily herself, but she'd raised five kids and was a font of knowledge. A few months with her would be the equivalent of a PhD in parenthood. Since he'd never expected to be a father, and since he'd only met his eighteen-month-old daughter three days ago, he needed the education. Badly.

The door opened, startling Lily into silence.

But it wasn't Gramma on the other side. It was... No. That wasn't possible.

"Evan?" The blonde woman squinted. "Is that you?"

Vanessa. He stared at the person who'd taught him, by her actions, that women couldn't be trusted. "What are *you* doing here?" he asked.

Lily wound up and let out an impressive wail, right in Evan's ear. As he winced and tried to bounce her into silence, he caught a glimpse of a big fluffy dog standing at Vanessa's side, leaning into her. It wore the red vest of a service dog.

"Come in, come in." At least, that's what he thought she said from reading her lips. Nothing was audible except Lily's wails.

Vanessa held open the door.

Evan stepped inside and looked at her more closely. Remembering the good times they'd had together made him want to smile and pull her into his arms. How long had it been, anyway? Eleven years? Twelve?

But they hadn't ended things on a hugging kind of note, and he had other concerns than his hormones and his heart now.

Vanessa reached for Lily, and without even thinking twice, he let her take the baby. Even Vanessa, who had the empathy of an ant, had to be better at childcare than he was.

She settled Lily on her hip and swayed gently. "Aren't you a pretty little princess?" She wiggled her fingers in front of the baby's face, patting her, somehow seizing her attention.

Lily's cries de-escalated.

"That's right," Vanessa crooned. "You're okay."

"Who is it, Mom?" A boy of about ten, blond like Vanessa, emerged from the kitchen, wiping his mouth with the sleeve of his hoodie.

Vanessa had a child?

"Declan, this is Mr. Dukas, Gramma Vi's grandson. Evan, this is my son, Declan." All the time she was speaking, Vanessa moved back and forth in a gentle rocking motion. She wore jeans and a loose-fitting sweater. Despite the heavy clothes, he could tell that she was even thinner than when he'd known her.

Still pretty, though. Very pretty.

Vanessa's son, Declan, greeted him politely. "This is Snickers," he added, kneeling and putting an arm around the service dog. "He's a Bernedoodle."

The name seemed to fit the brown, black and white, slightly goofy-looking dog. "Nice to meet you, Declan and Snickers," he said and then looked back at Vanessa. "Where's Gramma?"

Two vertical lines appeared between her eyebrows. "Gramma Vi is in the Chesapeake Corners hospital."

Evan froze. "What happened?"

"She fell. Day before yesterday, and she broke her wrist and her ankle. She's a little foggy on how it happened."

"Why didn't someone call me?" But he already knew why he wasn't at the top of the family's emergency list. His job took him to remote areas, and he was often without cell phone service. That was why his ex-wife had had such a hard time getting in touch with him about Lily, and why she'd been so hasty to hand him the baby and bolt when he'd finally gotten back to Philly.

He'd called Gramma within hours of getting Lily. They'd exchanged messages about his visit, so she knew he was coming. But that must have been before she'd fallen.

"Your uncle's listed as her emergency contact. He's been here off and on, but he had to drive back to Virginia today. So it's good you're here." Vanessa put a hand on his arm.

"Your gramma's doing well, Evan. Rehab will be serious, but she's ready to fight."

Her touch heated his blood. Unclear whether it was anger or attraction, but neither was relevant. He shook off her hand and the feeling. He needed to focus on Gramma. At her age, no illness or injury was minor.

Suddenly, Vanessa seemed to notice that they were all standing in Gramma's entryway. "Come on into the kitchen and sit down."

She was inviting him into his own grandmother's house, the house he'd grown up in. That was all kinds of wrong, but he pressed his lips together and followed her, his mind methodically clicking through next steps.

If Gramma couldn't help him, if she was in need of help herself, he'd have to hire someone to care for Lily on a part-time basis. And he had to do it fast. He couldn't visit Gramma at the hospital with a crying baby in tow. "Do you mind holding her another few minutes? I'm going to need to make some calls."

"No problem. We like babies." She sat down on a kitchen chair. Her son knelt beside her, jiggling a stuffed hot dog toy in front of Lily. It looked like a dog toy, actually. Whatever. If it entertained Lily, he was grateful.

The shaggy dog sat on Vanessa's other side, panting.

Through his general confusion and fatigue, one question emerged. "What are you doing here in my grandmother's house, anyway?"

"I'm Gramma Vi's caregiver. More of a companion, really." She frowned. "Or, I was."

"We hafta move now," her son contributed. "Since Gramma Vi's not living here anymore."

Gramma Vi's not living here anymore. The phrase gutted Evan. He could almost picture his grandmother stirring the pot that simmered on the stove, turning to smile at him, ready to hear his after-school stories.

This house wouldn't be a home without her. Was she going to heal? She had to heal.

How was he going to cope without her until she did? His throat tight, he held up his phone and strode out of the room.

Nannies, Chesapeake Corners, MD. The Google search rendered three results for agencies.

All of which had similar messages on their voicemail. "Out until after Thanksgiving."

"Have a good holiday."

"Enjoy Thanksgiving weekend with your family."

He leaned back and surveyed Gramma's living room. Old-fashioned chairs and end tables, family photos on the walls. The smell was slightly musty, with an undertone of the rose-scented lotion Gramma wore.

It was home. Only it wasn't. Gramma wasn't here.

He shut his eyes for a minute, wondering what to do next.

He'd taken a partial leave from his job until after the holidays. Metallurgical engineering, his role in it, anyway, slowed down at this time of year. As long as he worked a few hours every morning, called in most days and took care of any major issues that came up, his team could handle the rest.

From the kitchen, he heard the voice of Vanessa's son and her responding laughter. He didn't hear Lily crying, and that was a relief.

Young Declan had said they had to move out, since Gramma didn't need a home caregiver anymore.

What Evan didn't understand was how the woman who'd raised him could have let Vanessa be her caregiver for any length of time.

Maybe Gramma hadn't been able to find anyone else. If

she'd told him, he would have helped her find someone, even if he'd had to move them here.

He walked back into the kitchen to find his daughter calmly eating a snack, laughing while the boy, Declan, made faces at her. The dog watched closely, clearly waiting for food to fall. Lily was sitting at the table, and he bent to see how they'd managed that. "You have a booster chair?"

"I found it in the attic. I think your cousins used it, way back. Will you join us for dinner?" She indicated the extra place she'd set at the table.

The last thing he wanted was to break bread with Vanessa. It seemed to indicate that he'd forgiven her and felt friendly.

Wrong on both counts.

But he was starving, and his innate practicality made him take advantage of her offer. He sat, and Declan said a short prayer, and they all dug in.

After a few bites of rich potato soup and warm bread, he reluctantly put down his spoon. "We need to work this out. You're actually living here?"

Vanessa nodded. Focused on cutting up cheese and grapes for Lily, she hadn't touched her own soup. "Yes. Your gramma said we could stay on until Christmas, but I'm trying to find another place sooner. It's not fair for us to stay when she won't be living here."

"She's moving out for good?" he asked sharply.

"That's up to her, but her doctors are urging her to consider assisted living, at least."

How had he not known this? Was he so far removed from Gramma's life that she hadn't thought to consult him about a major decision like where to live going forward?

Vanessa seemed to read his mind, and he remembered she'd been good at that. "She was going to call you, I think, but she's been pretty overwhelmed with the testing and surgery."

"Surgery?" Worse and worse.

"They had to fix her bones," Declan said. "She's got a cast, and she said I could sign it!"

Wait. This kid had talked to Gramma, and Evan hadn't?

Again, Vanessa seemed to read his mind. "Declan hasn't visited yet, but he spoke to her by phone. Did you get your calls made?" She poured a few crackers onto the table in front of Lily, along with the cheese and cut-up grapes.

"I'm trying to find a part-time nanny for Lily, but no agencies seem to be taking calls right now."

"Mom could be Lily's nanny," Declan said.

The words hung in the air. The play of expressions over Vanessa's face had to match his own: shock, disbelief and a very big *no*.

No way could he let Vanessa, who'd stomped so hard on his own heart, watch over his vulnerable daughter.

Vanessa's immediate reaction to her son's suggestion was a visceral *no way*. She read the same response in Evan's horrified expression.

"No, that wouldn't work," Evan said.

"I don't think so, honey," Vanessa said at the same time.

"Why not?" Declan asked. "He needs a nanny. You like babies." He paused, his expression going thoughtful. "And if you did that, we could stay here."

His plaintive tone was almost enough to make Vanessa consider the idea. Almost, but not quite.

Snickers had been lying beside her chair, his usual dinnertime position. Now, the Bernedoodle stood and leaned against her, his large body a comfort.

Declan looked back down at his soup bowl and pushed

a remaining chunk of celery around and around the bottom of it.

Poor kid. He didn't want to move, knowing that they'd likely have to find a place in another school district. He was only in fourth grade, but he hadn't had an easy time of it, given Vanessa's issues. He needed stability, and she was determined to provide it.

Only, part of that was to keep herself from getting too stressed out. Stress could send her right back into her eating disorder, and that was a risky place to be. Better a little discomfort on Declan's part than a complete meltdown on her own.

Even the thought of being near Evan Dukas on a daily basis, working for him, shot her stress level into the stratosphere. Evan was big and opinionated and way too good-looking. Moreover, the memory of their brief, just-for-the-holidays relationship twelve years ago made her cringe with embarrassment. She'd been a jerk, no question.

She placed her hand on Snickers's back and then met her son's hopeful eyes. With a quick headshake, she dashed what was left of his hopes.

He was such a good kid. He didn't make a fuss. He just kept pushing that piece of celery around his empty soup bowl.

Snickers nudged at her hand. When she didn't respond, he nudged her leg and gave a deep, sharp *woof*.

"Shh," she told him, looking over at the baby. Lily didn't seem to be afraid of dogs, but Snickers's bark was loud.

"He wants something to eat," Evan said.

"He wants *her* to eat," Declan said, nodding toward Vanessa.

Evan looked briefly puzzled, but Declan didn't elaborate.

Good. The last thing Vanessa wanted to do was discuss her psychiatric service dog with the best man she'd ever dumped.

She passed the salad around the table and then focused on her own bowl of soup, managing to eat more than half of it. The baby pounded a spoon against the table.

"Can I give her some bread and butter?" Declan asked Evan.

"Sure," he said.

Declan buttered a slice and then cut it into small pieces. He put several on the table in front of Lily, and she mashed them into her mouth.

"You seem comfortable with babies," Evan commented.

Declan nodded. "Mom babysits sometimes, and I help," he said. "That's why she'd be a good..." He trailed off.

"Dessert?" Vanessa said, forcing a bright tone into her voice. She couldn't imagine eating anything more herself, but both Evan and Declan had finished every bit of their soup, salad and bread. "We have cookies and ice cream."

"Sounds great," Evan said, and Vanessa remembered that he was, as Gramma always said, a hearty eater. When they'd been together and had enjoyed meals with his grandmother, he had always been willing to try new foods and had devoured whatever Gramma had served for dinner.

Vanessa got ice cream and scooped it into two bowls for Evan and Declan, then put a plate of cookies on the table. "Can the baby have a little ice cream?" she asked.

Evan shrugged. "Your guess is as good as mine," he said.

"What?" She stared at him. "She's your child, right?"

He reddened. "Yes. I'm 90 percent sure she is." He glanced at Declan, who looked as puzzled as Vanessa felt.

It didn't stop her son from scooping ice cream rapidly into his mouth, until he let his spoon clatter into the bowl and put his hands to the sides of his head. "Brain freeze," he yelled.

Vanessa laughed as she dished out a small amount of ice cream for the baby, then scooped tiny bites into her mouth. It would take the focus off the fact that she wasn't eating any, herself. Kids were good that way.

And that was her old pattern of thinking, she reminded herself. Hiding what she was and wasn't eating from those close to her. She felt her heart rate accelerate.

She touched Snickers's back and looked at Declan. "Do you have homework?"

"No. Well...a little."

"Go do it," she told him. "It can't be much, since tomorrow's the day before Thanksgiving break. Get it done, and then you can watch some TV." Surely Evan wouldn't expect them to move out tonight.

Surely he didn't intend to stay the night here, himself.

Declan groaned and left the room.

Only then did she realize how much of a buffer her son had been. Now, with the baby eating pieces of cookie Evan had broken off for her, the air between them felt charged. She stole a glance at Evan to find him looking at her.

Her heart raced again. She took a deep breath and went on the offensive. "How come you don't know what the baby can eat, or whether she's yours?"

He put down his spoon and wiped his mouth, and she had the feeling he was figuring out what to say. She waited, not pushing him. He didn't like to be pushed, she remembered that.

"I, well, I didn't know I had her until she was dropped off with me three days ago," he said.

She blinked. "Dropped off by whom?"

"My ex-wife," he said. "I didn't realize, when we divorced two years ago, that she was pregnant."

"What? Why didn't she tell you?" Vanessa remembered

her own journey. It hadn't been easy to tell Declan's father that she was expecting his baby, but that had been one of her first priorities, even so.

"That's a good question," he said. "We didn't exactly part on good terms. Still, I would have thought she'd want child support. The fact that she didn't ask for it...well, that's the 10 percent of why I'm not sure Lily is mine."

The words were spoken in Evan's calm, measured way, but his eyes looked a little...flat. If his wife had left him, and she was pregnant, and he didn't know still if the baby was his...the only reason could be that he didn't think she was faithful to him.

Ouch. She started to reach out a hand to him, wanting to pat his arm, and then pulled it back.

He didn't look like he'd welcome sympathy, not from her, anyway. Of course not. He had plenty of reason to be angry at her.

She stood and started clearing dessert dishes, glad for the chance to lower the intensity of their discussion. It was always better to have something to do with your hands. "So you brought her here?" she asked. "You weren't planning to leave her with Gramma, were you?"

"No!" He looked shocked. "Gramma's ninety. I knew she couldn't take care of a baby, even before... Oh, man. I'm really worried about her."

"She's all right for now," Vanessa assured him as she opened the dishwasher. "You'll want to see her for yourself, and you probably can tomorrow. But the doctors are talking positively, and she seems to feel pretty good."

"I'll visit tomorrow and talk to her doctors," he said. "But no. I wasn't planning to ask her to assume any care of Lily. I have partial paternity leave from work, and I plan to do most of the caregiving. It's just... I know nothing about babies in general, or Lily in particular. As you saw, I don't even know what she can eat."

He sounded discouraged.

"Your ex didn't leave any instructions?"

"Nothing I could make much sense of," he said. "I have Lily's medical records and a couple handwritten pages about her schedule. I was so shocked, though, that I didn't know the right questions to ask."

His shoulders slumped. He looked well and truly overwhelmed.

She hated to see it. One of the qualities she'd most liked in Evan, when she'd known him before, was his confidence. A smart, steady science nerd with confidence.

Apparently, that didn't extend to fatherhood, at least the first week of it.

Compassion filled her. Parenting was complicated in the best of circumstances. "You'll figure it out. And Gramma will be happy to give advice. She likes to stay busy and help people. She'll be so excited. Her great-grandchild!"

"Yeah. She'll like that." He grabbed the sponge and started wiping off the table.

It made her remember that he'd lived here for many years. He knew where Gramma kept everything. More so than Vanessa, who'd only been living here with Gramma Vi the past six months.

"Chesapeake Corners is a good place to raise a child," she said, unsure of why she so wanted to cheer Evan up. "You'll find lots of help here."

"Not a nanny, though," he said. "At least not quickly."

"No. Not on a holiday weekend." She was tempted to tell him that childcare was expensive and hard to find even outside the holiday season. But he already seemed so discouraged.

He came over to the sink and rinsed the sponge, glancing at her. "The idea that you could be Lily's nanny is just..."

"Ridiculous?" she supplied. Especially since the man seemed uncomfortable just being in the same room with her. And being in the same room together made her own stress level rise to the point where Snickers sensed it. The dog was sticking to her side like glue.

"Right. Ridiculous. And I don't see us living together here like one big happy family, so... You said you were planning to move out during the holidays?"

Her stomach lurched. "Yes. I'm trying to figure that out." She looked at the Thanksgiving decorations she'd put up on the windowsill above the sink, the cheerful turkey salt and pepper shakers on the table.

Snickers whined and nudged his big head under her hand.

"Seems like we're both in a bind," Evan said. He seemed to be thinking out loud as he started wiping down the countertops. "There are probably a few vacancies at the Baywater Inn, but being in one room with an eighteen-month-old means I couldn't call in to my office. And when she cries... the other guests would hate it."

She nodded. "Doesn't sound like a good option."

"What about you? Do you have anywhere you could move on short notice?"

She turned and leaned back against the counter. "I could move in with my brother and his wife. They'd make room for me. But they have three new foster kids and they're trying to bond as a family. Adding me and Declan to the mix wouldn't work real well. We actually lived in their carriage house for a while, but when I got this gig six months ago, their housekeeper moved into it."

Lily started verbalizing, doing those cute "ah-ba-BEE-ba"

syllables that sounded like conversation, though the words themselves were nonsensical.

"I don't know what she's trying to say." Evan went to the baby and ran a hand gently down her back.

"She's just practicing," Vanessa said, wanting to reassure Evan even though she was aware that most eighteen-month-olds had a bigger vocabulary than Lily had displayed. "She'll learn real words soon."

He nodded. Then he looked speculatively from the baby to Vanessa and back again. "So...since neither of us has another place to go, would you be willing to help out as her nanny, just through the Thanksgiving holiday?" His voice was tentative.

Vanessa froze. She gripped the counter with one hand. With the other, she stroked Snickers's head.

"I'd pay you whatever is fair," he said.

No, screamed everything in Vanessa. *Danger, danger, stay away.*

This entire evening had been stressful. Extending it into the long Thanksgiving weekend might just push her over the edge.

But Evan obviously needed help. He was in a real bind through no fault of his own. Little Lily needed a caregiver who knew something about babies.

As for avoiding stress...it wasn't possible, really, not now. Working for Evan would be stressful, but so would moving in with her brother. Moving herself and Declan into an apartment would be stressful. An increase in expenses would be stressful. She had a decent settlement from Declan's late father, but she was saving hard to make sure she could provide Declan with school enrichment activities and hockey equipment and, ultimately, a good college education.

She let her eyes rest on Evan. Let the memories come.

How exquisite it had been to be with him. What a wholesome vision of how life could be.

In the end, she'd realized it could never work between them, and she'd backed away.

It was a vision that would never come to reality for her. But maybe, for a few days, while she looked for another place to live...

She looked up at the ceiling, toward Declan's room. He would be thrilled at the chance to stay here, even for a little while longer. He loved Gramma's place, with its edge-of-town location, its proximity to the Chesapeake Bay, its big yard all his friends liked to come play in.

The house's layout offered privacy. Gramma had a bedroom, sitting room and bathroom here on the first floor, while she and Declan occupied the second floor. So Evan and Lily *could* stay in Gramma's part of the house.

Taking care of Evan's baby, working for Evan...yes, that was risky. But for Declan...well. She'd do anything for her son.

"Okay," she said with a sinking heart. "I'll do it."

Chapter Two

The day after arriving in Chesapeake Corners, Evan walked into his grandmother's hospital room practically holding his breath.

He was mentally prepared to see her in bed and hooked up to machines, or at least, he'd tried to prepare himself for that. Instead, she was sitting upright in a wheelchair, dressed not in a hospital gown but in black sweat pants and a red button-down shirt.

He tapped on the edge of the door. "Gramma?"

Her face lit up and she held out a hand, and he went to her and gave her a gentle hug. Then he pulled a chair close to hers. "You look good," he said. Then he spotted the cast on her wrist and the orthopedic boot on her foot.

"I'm in good shape for the shape I'm in," she said. Her laugh and happy demeanor almost made him cry with relief.

"Tell me what happened," he said. "Catch me up. I wish you'd called me."

She waved her good hand. "A little fall," she said. "Would've been nothing in my sixties or seventies, but now that I'm the big nine-oh, seems like things hit me a little harder."

"I'm sure they do. What do the doctors say?"

"They say I'm old. As if I didn't know it! Now, tell me about you. How was your trip? Did the baby do okay?"

Again, he was relieved. From what Vanessa had said, Gramma had fallen the day after he'd called and let her know he and Lily were coming. He hadn't been sure that she would remember what he'd told her.

It looked like he wasn't going to get a lot of medical details from Gramma. That was typical of her. He'd call the doctor later today and see if he could learn more about the true state of her health and her needs.

"Where *is* the baby?" Gramma asked.

"Lily's downstairs with Vanessa," he said. Her name tasted strange in his mouth. It was the first time he'd said it out loud in twelve years.

"That's wonderful! The two of you are getting along, then?"

Were they? He guessed they were, although it was an awkward situation for both of them.

"I want to see the baby," she said. "Take me downstairs."

"No. It's not safe for you to go running around the hospital."

"I'm in a wheelchair, but I'm supposed to move and exercise. And keep my spirits up. Seeing my great-granddaughter is just the ticket."

Hoping to distract her from what seemed like a dangerous plan, he changed the subject. "I was surprised to find Vanessa there," he said. "As well as her son. Did you... Do you actually want them living with you?" He was so accustomed to thinking of Vanessa as a bad person that he'd wondered, in the wee hours, whether she'd somehow coerced Gramma into taking her and her son in.

"Oh, yes," Gramma said. "I love having them there. Vanessa is wonderful, and that son of hers, Declan, is a real good boy. Reminds me of you when you were that age." She narrowed her eyes. Studied him intently.

It made him uncomfortable. "What?" he asked.

"Is Declan yours, or could he be?"

"Gramma!" Evan's face heated. "No. There's no way." He and Vanessa had been attracted to each other, very much so. Their Christmastime relationship had been short but intense. They'd never been intimate, though. Evan wasn't the type to jump into a close relationship quickly, and Vanessa had seemed to appreciate his restraint.

Seemed being the operative word. In the end, she'd brushed him off like you'd flick away an annoying bug. And apparently gotten together with someone else soon afterward.

"Oh. Too bad. There's some kind of mystery around Declan's father, and I thought I might have it solved."

He reached down and retrieved a slipper that had fallen off. Carefully, he put it on her unbooted foot. "Did you *want* me to be Declan's father?" The notion shocked him. "I thought you believed in..." He trailed off, not wanting to say it.

"Oh, Evan." She patted his arm. "Of course I would urge anyone to stay out of intimate relationships until marriage. I'm glad if you managed to do that. But if you'd made a mistake, and it had resulted in a beautiful, wonderful child... I'd have forgiven you in a heartbeat."

He looked away, embarrassed to be discussing such things with his grandmother. He knew he was a little rigid in his beliefs, but come on. He'd done the right thing.

"Anyway," Gramma went on, "Vanessa is a lovely young woman. I'm glad you're going to spend more time with her."

Evan frowned. Had Gramma somehow set him up to come stay with Vanessa while she was recuperating? Was that why she hadn't mentioned her live-in companions when he'd called her in a panic about Lily?

"Right now," she said, "I'm imagining what that baby of yours looks like. Take me down, will you?"

Evan wanted out of this small, confining, disinfectant-smelling room. He could understand why Gramma wanted out, too. "You're sure it's okay with your doctors?"

"It's fine," she said, waving her good hand.

So he pushed her to the elevator, and soon they approached the hospital lobby. Gramma held up a hand. "Stop a minute," she said quietly. "Look."

Vanessa sat by the window, Lily in her arms. She was looking down at the baby with every evidence of fondness, and Lily was reaching up to touch her face.

They looked like mother and daughter.

Maybe because Gramma had asked if Vanessa had borne his child, the sight of his baby in her arms caused a squeeze to Evan's heart.

What would it be like if he and Gramma were approaching his wife and child right now? If Vanessa were his wife, and the baby was theirs together?

It would cause you pain when she dumped you and the baby. Shaking off his idealized, unrealistic daydream, he pushed the wheelchair forward.

Vanessa looked up, spotted Gramma and rose to greet her, the baby in her arms. Soon Gramma was holding the baby, with Vanessa on one side and Evan on the other, both poised to whisk Lily away if she got restless or proved too much of a handful for Gramma.

"How are you doing?" Vanessa touched Gramma's arm. "I've been so worried about you. Are you feeling okay?"

"I've been better," Gramma admitted. "Physically, that

is. Emotionally, I'm just thrilled to have my boy back home, and extra thrilled he brought this little sweetheart."

"Good. I'm glad to see you, but I think we should keep this visit short. This is a lot of excitement for you."

"We can keep it short," Gramma said, tilting her head to one side, "but I'd like to come home for Thanksgiving dinner."

Vanessa glanced at Evan. "I don't think they'll be ready to release you today or tomorrow. And when you leave the hospital, your doctors want you to go to a rehab place for a little while."

Gramma looked pleadingly at Evan. "See how overprotective she is? You'll bring me home for Thanksgiving, won't you?"

"Absolutely not," he said.

"Miss Vi!" A nurse came bustling over. "I've been looking all over for you. You know you're not supposed to leave the floor."

Gramma's eyes twinkled. "I must not have heard that restriction. Look at my beautiful great-grandbaby!"

"She's a doll," the nurse said, "but we all know that babies carry a lot of germs around with them. We don't want you exposed to that until you're stronger."

Gramma rolled her eyes. "Treating me as if I'm made of glass. All right, all right."

"I'll come visit you tomorrow, Gramma," Evan promised. Then he looked at Vanessa. "That's if you'll be able to take care of the baby for a couple of hours. We haven't pinned down those kind of details yet."

"Of course," Vanessa said easily. "I'm going to cook a small Thanksgiving dinner at the house, but it'll be early-ish. You can leave her and visit Gramma, and if you're not back I'll take her with Declan and me to visit my brother and his family. If that's okay."

"Sounds good." Evan had no idea what was okay and what wasn't, for a baby, so he figured it would be better to defer to Vanessa's greater knowledge.

"I'm planning to visit the grocery today," Vanessa went on. "Gramma Vi, I can pick you up some of those cookies you like, and Evan will bring them."

"Wonderful," Gramma said. She beckoned for Evan to move closer as Vanessa spoke with the nurse. "You take care of Vanessa, too, do you hear me?"

"Um, okay." Was this more matchmaking on Gramma's part?

"I mean it. She isn't as strong as she looks. She'll need help with the shopping and cooking."

"Okay." Evan didn't want to get into an extended conversation with the nurse looking on, intent on taking Gramma back to her room.

"Promise me?"

"Yes." He kissed her. And realized he'd just committed to spending even more time with Vanessa.

Grocery stores had never been Vanessa's favorite places. Going to one with Evan and his baby did nothing to make it easier. People kept stopping to greet Evan. Who knew he was so popular in town? And Lily seemed to arouse everyone's curiosity as they tried to figure her out. Was she Evan's? Vanessa's? Theirs together?

She took deep breaths, longing for Snickers's comforting presence even though he, too, tended to draw attention. She'd elected to leave him at home because she'd felt that both a baby and a dog visiting the hospital would be too much.

She hadn't realized the visit would last as long as it had.

They'd decided to stop at the grocery store on the way home. So now her goal was to make this snappy, pick up Declan from school and get home without too much stress.

Inside, shoppers crowded the produce section and argued with one another about what size of turkey to buy. A silver-haired man nudged another with his cart, leading to a sharp exchange. Prepared food lent an odor of grease and overcooked vegetables to the crowded store.

"We're going to have to hustle so we can pick up Declan in time," Vanessa told Evan. "Let's hit produce first."

He nodded, but she wasn't sure he'd heard what she had said. He looked confused. Overwhelmed.

"Didn't you ever go to a grocery store before?" she asked him.

"Of course I did! But...not often. I mostly shop at a local corner market. And I get takeout a lot." He looked around. "Is it always this crowded?"

"Day before Thanksgiving," she explained. "Which is a cooking holiday, so everyone's picking up last-minute stuff. Like us."

She had a sudden memory of stopping in this very grocery with him, during their brief relationship. She'd wanted to get out, and he'd suggested a winter picnic. They'd picked up soup and sandwiches and hot chocolate, and he'd driven them to a local campground and built them a fire.

It had been sweet and romantic, and they'd shared their first peck of a kiss.

While she'd been lost in memories, Evan had drifted over to the cranberry display. He picked up a bag of fresh cranberries, and then a can from the side of the display. He studied both, looking puzzled. Lily was propped on his hip, surveying the bustle with interest. Vanessa could already see that, like Declan, Lily enjoyed the people-energy. She was a budding extrovert, it seemed.

Vanessa was about to approach Evan and get him on track when a woman came over to him, giving him an appreciative once-over. Evan had nerd vibes, with his glasses and white button-down shirt. But he was also built, with broad shoulders obvious even through his coat. She'd never considered it before, but he must be popular with women.

"Do you like fresh or canned?" the woman asked. She glanced down at Evan's ringless left hand, then smiled and stepped closer.

"Um...what's the difference?" He barely looked at her, still studying the can versus the bag.

"Oh, fresh are the best by far," she said. "What a cute baby! How old is she?"

"Eighteen months," Evan said abstractly.

"Just like my Emma!" The woman gestured to the baby in her cart. "Oh, you want down, sweetie, don't you?" She set her baby on the floor, and the little girl toddled toward a display of apples with clear intent. "App-uh," she said, reaching out for them.

The woman rushed to grab her before she started to climb onto the display. She looked back at Evan, but he'd turned away and walked toward Vanessa.

It was kind of cute how he didn't realize she'd been trying to hit on him.

Vanessa watched the other woman's baby point and speak and toddle, and she realized that she was way ahead of Lily developmentally, even though they were apparently the same age. Hmm. She could probably mention it to Evan. Not now, when they were in a hurry, but soon.

It would upset him, though, and was that really her responsibility? She was just the temporary nanny.

An Unexpected Christmas Helper

She reached Evan's side, and they both backed close to a shelf of breads and wraps, trying to get out of the way of the bustling shoppers around them. "I didn't even do a background check on you," he said suddenly.

Really, he was bringing that up in a busy grocery store? "I've never broken the law," she said truthfully.

Except a moral one, with Declan's father.

"Anyway, this nanny thing is just temporary," she told Evan as Lily started to fuss. "Let's focus on getting through our list and out of here."

"That makes sense." He swayed with Lily, awkwardly. Did not make a move toward actual shopping.

Realizing she would have to give Evan specific directions, she said, "Go get us two heads of broccoli and a bag of potatoes."

"Uh, with the baby?"

Vanessa was torn between laughing and praying for strength. "Someone has to hold the baby while we shop."

"Oh. Right." He turned.

Lily's fussing turned into cries.

Vanessa took the baby from him. "Go," she said, pointing toward the fresh vegetable display.

She jiggled Lily and swayed, tried putting her in the seat of the cart, and then found crackers to feed her in her diaper bag. But the baby was inconsolable. She'd probably missed her afternoon nap and was off schedule.

Her cries rose to earsplitting level. People stared. Vanessa's heart rate accelerated.

Evan wove his way back to her. He held two loose heads of broccoli in one hand and a huge bag of potatoes in the other. Way too many for their little gathering, but she wasn't going to split hairs now with a screaming baby in her arms.

He dumped his finds in the cart and frowned at Lily. "What's *wrong* with her?" he asked.

"She's a baby, she cries," Vanessa snapped. And then it clicked for her. "Also, she's grieving her mother, right? She never knew you before." They were actually pressed against the bread display now as people tried to squeeze past them.

When there was a break, Vanessa handed the baby to Evan and led the way toward the meat section.

Evan followed along. "I think my ex-wife left her with caregivers a lot," Evan said over Lily's fussy cries. "Apparently she got into a relationship with someone who didn't like kids."

So that was her excuse for abandoning her baby with someone who, while allegedly her father, knew nothing about kids. "I don't think I could have left Declan with someone else for long," she said.

Except with her brother when she was losing it with anorexia.

But at least he'd been a stable person and well-known to Declan. Her brother was still a big part of Declan's life. Though not as big lately, as busy as he was with his new foster kids.

"You know," she said, "if Lily had a lot of caregivers, that's not the best, either. Do you know if it was a stable situation?" She rummaged in the diaper bag, found a Binky and popped it in Lily's mouth. Immediately, the baby quieted.

"She just said caregivers, plural," Evan said.

People were crowding around the turkeys, discussing the merits of fresh versus frozen, real meat thermometers versus the plastic pop up ones already inserted into the bird's flesh.

Yuck.

Vanessa grabbed a fresh turkey and stuck it in the cart. "I figure Gramma Vi has a meat thermometer," she said.

"You're a cute couple," a young mom said. "I love how you're actually talking with each other instead of arguing."

Vanessa glanced at Evan. His neck had turned red.

And why did she know to watch for that particular tell?

Vanessa's phone chimed, and she pulled it out of her purse. Declan. She took the call. "Everything okay?"

"Are you coming to pick me up?" he asked.

Her eyes widened. How long had they been here? "Yes, I'm coming, but I'm stuck at the store," she said. "It'll be half an hour. Just sit tight."

"You're there with that guy and baby?"

"Um, yes."

"Fine," he said. She heard him speak to someone else.

At least, she thought so; the call was hard to hear over the voices and announcements at the store. "What?" she asked.

"Caleb's grandma said she'd bring me home."

"Tell her thank you, and go right in the house," she said.

Declan ended the call without saying goodbye.

She pressed her lips together. She felt like a bad mom. He, Evan, had made her a bad mom. He was a distraction she didn't need.

Her heart raced and her breathing quickened. She reached a hand down instinctively, then remembered that Snickers was at home.

"This...might not work," she said to Evan.

It definitely wouldn't work once the holiday weekend was over. She just prayed she could get through that so as to keep her word to Evan.

The store crowd seemed to press in on her. She took deep breaths.

Lily spit out her Binky and wailed.

Vanessa handed her list to Evan. "Get this stuff," she said. "Give me the car keys. I'm taking her out to wait in the car."

He took the list and squinted at it as if it were written in Greek. "Okay?" he said tentatively.

She'd make do with whatever food he got. Anyway, he could probably find some woman to help him decipher her list and purchase the items.

It was definitely going to be a long Thanksgiving weekend.

Chapter Three

Thanksgiving.

Evan hadn't thought too much about the holiday in recent years. He'd worked so much, and his wife had been busy, too, so they'd mostly eaten out. Nice dinners, but not exactly homey. After the divorce, he'd felt pathetic eating out alone, so he'd usually gotten takeout and just worked through the holiday. Either that, or he'd been overseas where American Thanksgiving wasn't celebrated.

Now, late morning, the smell of roasting turkey and pecan pie tickled his nose, calling to mind his grandma's holiday dinners. They'd usually had a whole table full of people there: singles, small families who'd transplanted to the area, immigrants who didn't know much about the holiday and wanted to learn. Gramma had been generous that way.

He lounged on the couch with Lily on his chest. Declan was in the recliner, and the dog, Snickers, lay sprawled on the floor.

It was relaxing. Fun. He hated to think of how this holiday would be had he gutted it out in DC, alone with Lily.

He looked at his daughter, clad in bright flowered overalls with a T-shirt in a completely different pattern underneath. She was barefoot because she wouldn't keep socks or shoes on her feet.

Was it true, what Vanessa had said yesterday? Was Lily grieving the absence of her mother?

Maybe he should try to arrange some kind of visitation with Frederika. But that wasn't happening anytime soon. She'd told him she'd be out of touch for a few weeks, traveling in Europe with her new flame.

He had to learn to care for Lily himself. He was getting better at changing diapers, and bathing her, and getting her dressed...although sometimes, like now, his fashion sense left something to be desired. He was finding ways to entertain her, simple stuff like holding his hands in front of his face and then pulling them away, or putting on comical expressions to make her laugh. He did that now.

Vanessa was helping a lot. Gramma would help him, too, he hoped. He'd called her this morning and was planning to go over, later in the day. She'd gotten involved in a hospital activity with other patients and would be busy until midafternoon.

Typical Gramma.

He heard Vanessa talking in the kitchen and tried not to eavesdrop. The conversation seemed one-sided, so most likely, she was on the phone. Then he heard a male voice. She'd put her phone on speaker.

Did she have a boyfriend? He hadn't seen evidence of one, but it would be strange if someone as pretty as Vanessa didn't date. Maybe this call was about that. Maybe the guy would come over, join them for dinner. Evan was curious and a little disgruntled at the thought.

He refocused on the TV parade, pointing out to Lily a giant inflatable of one of the baby shows she liked. Then he put her down on a blanket on the floor and propped a mobile over her, for her to bat at. When he thought about it, it was strange that his ex hadn't brought many toys. From the research he'd been doing late at night, it seemed like Lily should have active toys, push toys and bouncy toys, as well as blocks and such to stimulate her brain.

Hopefully, she'd had those things and Frederika had just been too busy to pack them up.

Maybe she hadn't packed them because she was thinking about taking Lily back once her fling had ended.

He put a possessive hand on his daughter's back. Now that he knew about her, he wasn't letting her go, no way. Frederika could visit, but he was going to be the main parent if humanly possible.

Vanessa came through the door, wiping her hands on a dish towel. "Bad news, Declan. Luke and Angie got a last-minute call that their kids' birth parents want a visit today. They have to drive into the city, so we'll need to postpone our dinner with them until later in the weekend."

"Aw, man!" Declan threw down the ball he'd been tossing from hand to hand. "This day is gonna be no fun at all."

"I know you're disappointed," she said. "I am, too. But we'll manage. We always do."

Declan blew out a disgusted breath. "This stinks, and it's your fault. You never have anything fun for me to do. Our house is boring." He added a mild expletive and then lifted his chin as if daring Vanessa to comment on it.

"Hey," Evan snapped. "Don't talk to your mother that way."

"Who are you to tell me what to do?" Declan sneered.

Evan saw Vanessa suck in a deep breath and straighten her shoulders. Her dog trotted over to stand beside her, and she rested her hand on its shaggy head. "Your language and attitude are unacceptable, Declan. I'd like for you to go outside and pick up all the sticks in the yard. Bundle them for the trash."

"I don't know how," he groused.

"You do know how. There's twine in the garage. I expect you to do it right."

"Awww!" Declan stood and stomped off through the kitchen.

Lily watched the proceedings, wide-eyed.

"Sorry if I made it worse," Evan said. "Mind if I go out and help him? It'll mean you have to watch Lily, though."

She shrugged. "I'm her nanny. I'm glad to watch her. I've got everything started that I can start." She came over and sat by Lily, picking up a scarlet stuffed crab toy and making it dance in front of her. "You know, you really ought to get this child some more toys. It's just sad she has to play with this disgusting thing."

"Dog toy?" he guessed.

"Uh-huh." She sniffed it and grimaced. "I'll root around and see if I can find something better for her to play with. Go on, go outside. It's actually pretty nice out for Thanksgiving Day."

She was right. Evan pulled on a sweatshirt and went out into the breezy fifty-degree day. Weak sunshine illuminated the brown-green grass and the piles of leaves.

Declan walked around picking up sticks and throwing them, hard, into a pile beside the garage.

Probably a good way to get his frustrations out. Evan took the other side of the yard and started picking up sticks and tossing them, more gently, to the same spot.

A few minutes later, when he was in earshot of Declan, he spoke. "I have no say over what you do. But it seems like your mom works hard and deserves respect."

A gust of wind swirled the dead leaves around their feet. Declan looked at the ground. "Yeah," he mumbled after a minute.

Evan was about to start bundling sticks when the boy spoke again. "My uncle used to do stuff with me. I stayed at his place all the time. Now he's *too busy*." Declan said the last two words in a mocking tone, making exaggerated air quotes with his fingers.

"That's rough." Evan remembered his own childhood, how he'd yearned for time with his dad and didn't get it. "Hand me that twine?"

They tied up bundles of sticks in silence, the sun warm, the smell of damp leaves and pine needles filling the air. Finally, they stacked the bundles at the curb.

Evan saw one of those bright rubbery toy footballs, half tucked beneath a bush. He picked it up, shook dirt off it and tossed it sideways to Declan.

Declan caught it and tossed it back. "I have a real football in the garage," he said, looking hopefully at Evan.

"Get it." Evan juggled the Day-Glo football from hand to hand while Declan ran into the garage. A moment later the boy emerged with a standard-sized football. "Catch," he yelled with a decent approximation of a bullet toss.

Evan caught it. "Go out for a long one," he said, gesturing, and Declan took off. Evan did a couple of warm-up swings and then threw the football so that it landed perfectly in Declan's arms.

They played like that for a while. Neighbors were out, too; a football overthrown led to a cordial holiday conversation with updates on Gramma.

Vanessa came out on the porch, holding Lily. Beside them trotted Snickers, and they all sat down, Vanessa on the bottom step with Lily on her lap, and Snickers on the ground.

Evan was watching her so hard that the football Declan tossed bonked him on the head.

"Ow," he complained, still watching Vanessa.

She smiled. "Dinner's ready," she called to Evan and Declan.

Now her dog was barking at her and tugging her jeans with his teeth. "How come the dog is doing that?" he asked Declan.

"It's time for Mom to eat," Declan explained.

Strange. He wanted to know more about Vanessa's service dog's role in her life. He was tempted to ask Declan about it, but it wouldn't be right to put a child in the middle. If he had a question for Vanessa, he should go directly to the source. He'd watch her and the dog throughout the Thanksgiving meal, and if he couldn't figure it out, he'd just ask her.

Half an hour later, he gave up on any but the most cursory effort to understand Vanessa's relationship with her dog.

He dug into succulent, moist turkey, creamy mashed potatoes with gravy, green beans and buttered rolls and stuffing. In between bites that almost made him groan with their deliciousness, he fed Lily tidbits of food.

She smacked her lips and babbled, the sound "Muh! Muh!" being predominant.

"I think she's saying 'more,'" Vanessa said.

Evan paid attention, and it was true: when he stopped feeding her, she demanded "Muh!" "She's talking!" he marveled.

"Yes. Now, cut up some turkey real small and let her feed herself. She should be able to eat some green beans, too, on her own."

"Right on the tray?" It seemed like a messy proposition.

"Yep." Vanessa frowned. "She should be using a spoon herself by now, or at least starting to. But I don't think she's learned to do that yet."

"Why not?" Evan frowned. Was she slow at learning, or hadn't Frederika taught her to use a spoon?

The dog, who'd been lying at Vanessa's side, lumbered to his feet and put his big head in Vanessa's lap.

"I know, I know," she said, seemingly to the dog. She took up her fork and started eating the plate of food before her.

All of a sudden, it dawned on him: she might have an eating disorder. But if so, was that a service-dog type of issue? And did it make her a bad candidate as a nanny?

He was going to have to ask her about it. And he was going to have to admit the reason why: he was liking the way Vanessa took care of Lily, and he was starting to wonder whether she'd be willing to continue all the way through the rest of the year.

The eating disorder question was one thing to resolve.

The other was that he kept forgetting what he knew: that Vanessa was someone who'd stomped on his heart once, that she was unreliable like most women, and that he needed to keep some sort of emotional distance between them.

After putting Lily down for a nap, Vanessa dropped into the recliner. She hadn't slept well and was grateful for a break.

Evan came into the living room. "I need to talk to you," he said.

She held back a sigh and put down the book she'd been planning to relax with. If this arrangement were longer term, she'd definitely need to set some boundaries. But it was only for the holiday weekend, so she'd be polite. "What's up?"

"Is Declan around?" he asked, sinking down onto the couch kitty-corner from the recliner she'd chosen.

She pointed upstairs. "He's playing a video game in his room."

"Good," he said. "I want to know about your dog and your eating disorder." His tone was stern, almost parental.

She tilted her head to one side and stared at him. "Are you kidding me?"

"No. I need to understand."

Her heart pounded and her face felt hot. This wasn't something she talked about to most people, and she certainly didn't want to discuss it with Evan. "You realize you're asking intrusive questions about my private business, right?"

"I'm sorry," he said. "I wouldn't ask without reason. This is important."

"Why?"

Snickers came over and leaned against the side of the recliner, pushing his head under her hand. She stroked him and took deep breaths.

"I need to understand because you're caring for my daughter."

"For the holiday weekend! Do you think I'm going to corrupt her eating habits in four days?" She pressed her lips together, but she couldn't keep the words in. "Anyway, I think you have bigger concerns in regard to Lily's eating."

His eyes widened. "What do you mean?"

"Well." She shifted in her chair, tucking her feet beneath her, gently scratching behind Snickers's ears. "She can't eat with a spoon. She can't drink from a regular cup. Those are milestones she should have met by now, or at least, I think so. Declan was doing both at twelve months."

He blew out a breath. "Really?"

"It would be worth checking out. Especially since…" She broke off.

"What?"

"I mean, I'm not an expert…"

"Just say it, Vanessa," he snapped.

Either Evan's social skills had deteriorated, or she'd just been too crazy about him to mind his bluntness. Irritating.

But, most likely, he sounded mad because he was worried about his daughter. "She doesn't walk, which is probably fine," she said. "She could just be a late walker. But she should be pulling up to a stand, and she doesn't do that. I tried to get her on her feet this morning, and she just sat down again. It's like she doesn't have strength in her legs."

"Do you think something's wrong with her?" He leaned forward, elbows on knees, hands clasped. "I mean...she seems so bright and happy. But what do I know?"

The worry on his face made her want to reassure him. "She's probably fine. There's a huge variation of what babies can and can't do at any given age. But getting her checked out by a pediatrician wouldn't be a bad idea."

"I'll get on it next week. Can you help me find somebody?"

"Sure," she said, then couldn't resist adding, "I can help you out even though I have a service dog and an eating disorder."

He met her eyes. "Thank you. And I'm sorry I was rude about that. I just really want to know if you're okay as her caregiver, because..." He broke off and looked at the floor, then back at her. "Because I was thinking about asking you to keep up the gig longer, until the New Year."

There was a wail from the back of the house. Lily. They looked at each other, and then Evan stood. "I'll get her."

"You do that." She watched him as he headed to his and Lily's suite of rooms.

Evan wanted her to keep caring for Lily throughout the holidays.

It would be good in a lot of ways. She and Declan could stay here, rather than trying to find somewhere else to live. She'd continue getting paid at least as much as she'd been making working for Gramma Vi.

And she loved babies. Lily was sweet and adorable, and Vanessa felt for her, being dumped by her mother and possibly neglected in terms of medical attention she might need.

It would be ideal, except for Evan. The man stressed her out. He was way too blunt, and skeptical about her, and seemed to consider her a questionable person. To live in the same house with a judgmental man could throw her back into her eating disorder. She already felt that telltale tension in her stomach, that feeling of wanting to be empty and in control. Snickers obviously sensed it, too; he was sitting in front of her now, his shaggy body pressed against her shins.

Should she go or stay? Neither option was great. She didn't even know if she *had* the option to stay, because Evan seemed to be making it contingent on her discussing her own personal health concerns—her *mental* health concerns, because that was what eating disorders were. She hated that he felt entitled to nudge his way into her brain and her business.

She let her head fall into her hands and tried to pray. But even that she wasn't good at. She didn't know if asking God to help her with this problem was legitimate, and if it was, how would she know His answer? Would He give an answer?

Her thoughts swirled and her tension mounted. This wasn't good. She slid to the floor, leaning back against the chair, her arm around Snickers.

She had to admit that Evan had a legitimate concern here. *Was* she suited to take care of a baby? Wasn't that her whole thing, that she had to overcome her eating disorder so that she could parent Declan properly?

Declan was her heart and her center, the most important thing in her life.

For Declan, getting to stay here, having a stable life in the house he'd been living in, would be a good thing. Even having Evan around might be good for him. He'd looked so happy earlier today, tossing the football with Evan. Having that new male influence for a month or two might help Declan adjust to his uncle's sudden lack of time to hang out.

Suddenly she realized she had her answer. She had to decide based on whatever was good for Declan. Staying here would be best for him, and in order to do that, she had to work as a nanny for Evan Dukas. If he'd have her.

Knowing that he was tenacious as a bulldog in researching facts, he wouldn't let go of this eating disorder question. And if she were going to stay on, it was legitimate for him to ask.

So she was going to pull herself together and tell him her story—at least the eating disorder part of it—and ask him, humbly, to keep her on as a nanny.

It had seemed to Evan that Vanessa wasn't willing to talk about her eating issues with him. Understandable. He wasn't her therapist, and he didn't have the right to be in her business.

But when he got home from visiting Gramma on Thanksgiving night, Vanessa was waiting for him.

She looked tense. And Snickers was right beside her, almost leaning on her. He'd already learned that meant she was stressed. Why?

"Is Lily okay?" he asked.

"She's fine. I just put her down, and she's really asleep, if I'm any judge of it. Short nap today and a lot of excitement."

He hung up his jacket and followed Vanessa into the living room. "Let's hope she sleeps through the night." In the four days he'd had her, she hadn't done that even once. No wonder. She'd been left with a stranger—her father—who was clearly inept at caring for her.

"Sit down," Vanessa said, and it sounded like an order. She

must have realized that herself, because she quickly added, "If you don't mind."

He sat. "What's up?"

"So, about my eating disorder." She sat in the wing chair across from him. Snickers flopped down beside her, leaning against her legs. "What do you want to know?"

"Uh…" She'd taken him off guard. "You're sure you want to talk about it?"

"I want the job you offered," she said, "so I'll tell you whatever you want to know."

She wanted the job. His heart lifted, but he tried to slow down, to think about what he needed to know in order to feel safe hiring her. "I guess, just the basics. When did it start, how bad did it get, and how are you now?"

Her forehead creased and she nodded. "Yeah. Okay. It started when I was in high school. I think I told you, back when we first met, that my brother, Luke, and I moved through a few different foster homes after our dad died."

"I do remember." He also remembered that she'd thrown out the fact like it had been a lot of fun and games, which of course it couldn't have been. He'd been too young, and too enamored of her, to consider that back then, but he saw it clearly now.

She took a sip of what looked like tea. "I was a regular size then, but like a lot of teenage girls, I thought I was too fat. Once I figured out that I could restrict my eating and get thin, I thought it was the best thing ever."

He frowned. "I'll admit I don't understand. Eating is such a pleasure to me."

"It used to be for me, too. Especially because we didn't always have enough food when Dad was alive. A good meal was a treat, but not anymore." She twisted one of the rings she was wearing, around and around on her finger. "I think I've ruined my chance of just simply enjoying food."

"But why—" He broke off. He needed to let her tell her story, her way.

She shifted in her chair and reached down to stroke Snickers's head. "Back then, I loved the feeling that I had control over something. My body, and then, well, boys' reactions to me."

He lifted an eyebrow. "You wanted to get boys' attention by not eating?"

"Well, by being thin." She gave a wry smile. "The sad thing is, it worked. For a while. Boys liked the girls who fit into size two jeans back then."

Evan didn't know what to say to that. It didn't seem like there was a right answer. He wasn't the best with women, but even he knew that discussing their weight with them was too loaded to be a win for anyone.

"Anyway," she continued, "I went too far with it. Got to where I was overly skinny. But I was a foster kid, so it wasn't…well, it wasn't really noticed that much, and it wasn't considered an issue. I didn't eat my family out of house and home the way my brother did. He actually got in more trouble about eating than I did."

"Didn't he notice you were getting too thin?"

"Not until he came back from overseas. He enlisted at eighteen."

Evan wasn't sure how to ask, but he wanted to know. "When we, uh, got to know each other before, were you having food issues? You seemed fine, but I can be oblivious."

One corner of her mouth lifted into a half smile. "You can be. But I was pretty good then, and it helped that you were…" She stopped, her face going pink.

He felt his breathing quicken. "I was what?"

She looked away. Looked back. "You were pretty...enthusiastic. Positive. About how I looked."

He smiled. "I was indeed." He was about to say "I still am," and then reality crashed in on him.

Yes, he'd liked how she looked. A lot. He'd also liked her fun demeanor, the way she teased him, the long talks they'd had so easily. He'd never been as comfortable with a woman, before or since.

He'd thought she felt the same way. And then she'd dumped him.

He wanted to ask why. Wanted to yell at her, hurt her the way she'd hurt him. Consciously, he relaxed his shoulders and took a breath before speaking. "So you were fine then. But afterward..."

"Afterward..." She paused and looked away. "I got back into disordered eating. Made some dumb mistakes." She flushed. "Got pregnant." She looked up again, her eyes going suddenly soft. "Not that Declan is a mistake. He's my heart."

Evan's hand tightened on the arm of the couch.

Who was the guy Vanessa had chosen after him? What had been his great appeal, such that she'd conceived a child with him? Why did she call Declan's father, at least, a mistake?

He wasn't a fan of big emotions. They caused nothing but trouble. Right now, though, they were rising up in him despite his effort to tamp them down.

Hurt. Anger. And, strangely, admiration. She had such a capacity for love, had so much love for her son.

Evan was starting to love Lily, but his love was mixed with frustration and confusion. He feared he'd never develop the sort of parental love that seemed to come to Vanessa so easily.

When he didn't ask more questions, she went on talking.

"I did manage to eat properly throughout my pregnancy, and Declan has been super healthy from birth. Afterward, though, I had some bad spells. Raising a baby alone was hard."

"His father didn't help you?" Evan nearly choked on the words.

"Not...not really. Not much." Her jaw tightened and she looked away.

"So you were on your own, raising him."

"My brother helped. At times, when I wasn't well enough to care for Declan, Luke took over caring for him." She lifted her chin. "About a year and a half ago, I got into serious therapy. Snickers was a part of that, and he's been a lifesaver." She buried her hand in the dog's thick fur. "I'm not going to say I'm cured. Eating disorders are..." She swallowed. "They're mental health issues, and relapse is common. But with the help of God and Snickers, and for Declan's sake, I'm determined to stay strong."

Reluctant admiration grew in Evan. She was working hard to deal with her issues for her son's sake.

She lifted her chin. "I do need to avoid stress, and that's my only concern with staying on as Lily's nanny."

"You think caring for a baby will cause too much stress?" Evan could believe that. He found fatherhood extremely stressful.

"No," she said. "I'd love to care for Lily. I think living here with you will stress me out."

He blinked. "Want to tell me why?"

She studied him steadily. "I have to be careful of my state of mind. I just don't know if I'm strong enough to be in the same house with someone who's judging me and my behavior and my choices every minute."

Her words stopped him, made him look inward. "Is that what I do?"

"I don't know," she said. "You sure seem to be judging me about my eating and my service dog. Which is fair," she added, holding up a hand. "You have to look out for your daughter and choose her the best possible caregiver. I get that."

He looked down at the floor. He didn't want to be judgmental, but apparently, that was how his behavior was coming off. He'd have to do some thinking about that. But as far as choosing a caregiver for Lily, he realized, *his* decision, at least, was made. "Gramma trusts you enough to have you as a caregiver. She had high praise for you when I visited her today. You seem to do great with Lily. So... I think... I would like to offer you the job as Lily's caregiver through the end of the year."

She raised an eyebrow. "Your hesitation being?"

He sucked in a breath. She'd been honest with him. He had to be honest with her. "You said it stressed you out to live here with me. I also find it a little taxing to live here with you, because of our past." He met her eyes. "As long as we're clear that this is a professional arrangement, and that there's no possibility of the two of us resuming the relationship we had before, it should be manageable."

Some emotion flashed in her eyes and then was gone. She held out a hand. "Deal."

He took her hand. Immediately, he remembered all the times they'd walked hand in hand, and how happy that had made him feel. He released the handshake quickly and stood. "I'll write up a contract just so we're clear on terms. Since caring for Lily is more labor-intensive than caring for Gramma, I'll pay you double what she was paying you."

An Unexpected Christmas Helper

Because he was so conflicted about her, he wanted to be ruthlessly fair.

Her eyes widened. "I can't deny that would be a big help, at Christmastime in particular. But you pay whatever you think is fair. We were getting by fine on Gramma's salary, since room and board were included."

"I'll pay you double," he said, and left the room before the emotions he felt, mingling with the feelings visible in her big gray-green eyes, undid him.

Chapter Four

Black Friday shopping. Vanessa loved it: the start of the Christmas season, the exuberant crowds, the excitement of getting a doorbuster deal.

Doing it with Evan today, though, might be a little different.

Vanessa got baby Lily out of the car seat while he pulled the stroller from the trunk. It was a good thing he *had* a stroller and car seat, at least. She'd been shocked at how little Evan possessed for the baby. No toys and precious few clothes.

Evan got the stroller unfolded, and Vanessa plunked Lily into it.

"Go ahead and fasten her in," she said.

He knelt and fumbled with the straps.

"No, pull the strap up between her legs and hook it to the one around her waist," Vanessa explained, demonstrating. Really, it was stunning how little Evan knew about childcare. How had Lily's mother been able to leave her child with someone so inexperienced?

But it was Evan. Super responsible Evan. The woman must have known that he'd figure it out, that he wouldn't let Lily be hurt or neglected on his watch.

While Evan got the wiggling baby strapped in, Vanessa let Snickers out of the car and breathed in the November air.

Clouds hung heavy in the sky and a cold wind blew. The

weather could have been depressing, but all the shops up and down Main Street were lit up and shoppers in bright coats crowded the sidewalks.

Vanessa was glad they'd dropped Declan off at her brother's. He'd be a lot happier shoveling snow and playing with the dogs there than he would have been if she'd dragged him along. She'd considered leaving Snickers home but didn't want to risk it. She needed the dog's reassuring presence if she were to spend the day with Evan.

Once they had Lily settled, Vanessa made sure Snickers's service dog vest was secured before they headed toward the toy store. He maneuvered the crowd easily, sticking close to her side while Evan pushed the stroller.

One happy little family. That was what someone from the outside might see.

When they reached the toy store, Evan opened the door and made as if to hold it for her, looked inside and then stepped back. "It's awfully crowded."

"Of course it is. It's Black Friday."

He pulled the stroller away from the entrance so a few more shoppers could go in. "Are you sure it's okay for her? Since she's, you know, delayed?"

Vanessa smiled. "We'll keep an eye on her, but stimulation is the best thing for babies. Do you know if she's been out and about a lot?"

"I know next to nothing about how she's been raised." He said the words in a clipped voice. A muscle twitched in his jaw.

"Let's see how she reacts." She stepped ahead of him and opened the shop door. "Forward, march."

He eased the stroller past her and Snickers and went inside, then waited for her and the dog to come in. "People do this on purpose?" he asked, hunching his shoulders a little as he looked around at the noisy, jostling crowd.

"They do. Believe it or not, I love Black Friday shopping." She knelt in front of the baby. "Now, we want to undo her jacket and wrap a little bit so she doesn't get hot. A hot baby is a fussy baby."

Evan watched, his expression skeptical. When a couple of excited shoppers nearly mowed him down on their way to the sale table, he backed flat against the wall.

She straightened and laughed at his deer-in-headlights expression. "This is nothing compared to a mall or a big-box store. Be glad you're only in a small-town shopping district. Come on, let's head for the baby toys."

As they walked through the store, a memory gripped her chest and squeezed. When she'd been pregnant with Declan, she'd come in here and walked around, looking at the toys she couldn't afford and wondering how she was going to manage motherhood, alone. What a lost, emotional child she'd been.

"You okay?" Evan asked.

She realized she'd stopped walking and flashed a smile up at him. "Just remembering."

"Do you come here often? This stuff's a little young for Declan."

"You're never too old for a toy store," she said lightly. She picked up a little wind-up train and showed it to Evan. "Wouldn't you love to find this in your Christmas stocking?"

His eyes darkened. "Last time I had a Christmas stocking was with you."

Oh. That long-ago Christmas morning came back to her, the romantic notes and silly doodads she'd put into a stocking for him. Obviously the wrong thing to bring up. She put the train back. "This way to the baby toys," she said, and speed-walked toward the back of the shop, Snickers beside her, gently nudging their way through the crowd.

Evan followed, and when they reached the toddler section, he looked around helplessly. "There's so much!"

He wasn't wrong. A floor-to-ceiling shelving unit held stuffies and wooden puzzles and plastic farms with sets of animals. Along the wall, colorful doll strollers and push lawn mowers were lined up beside little bicycles. A table held board books and rattles and bath toys.

"It's a lot," she admitted. "Let's look at the push toys. I think these would help encourage her walking. And look, here are some of those doorway jumpy seats."

"Jumpy seats." Evan tilted his head, studying the picture on the front of the box.

"You put the baby in and she bounces. It'll help her build up her leg strength." She saw that Lily was putting a plastic monkey into her mouth. "No, honey, put that down." She tugged it gently away.

Not gently enough. Lily let out a huge wail and reached for the monkey.

"Look, Lily!" Evan grabbed a sippy cup from the diaper bag and jiggled it in front of Lily.

She stopped mid-wail and held out her hands for it.

"Is this okay?" Evan knelt beside the stroller and looked up at Vanessa.

"Perfect!" she said, delighted. "You're learning fast."

They moved toward the back of the shop, Lily now quietly drinking from her cup. Vanessa knelt by a pink shopping cart. "When I was growing up, one of my friends had this for her little sister. I loved it and wanted it so much. These are evergreen."

Lily flung her cup aside and reached for the cart.

"Looks like Lily likes it, too." Evan picked up the cup, wiped the mouth of it on his shirt and handed it back to Lily.

Vanessa laughed. "You *are* learning fast," she said. "Come on, let's grab what you want from here and keep moving. I can tell our time is limited."

She took over the stroller while Evan collected the pink shopping cart, a package of plastic vegetables to go with it and the doorway bouncy chair. He was loaded down, so she and Snickers led the way, weaving through the shoppers.

When she saw a classic stacking ring toy, she just held it up, eyebrows raised. He nodded, and she tucked it under her arm. "She needs a doll, too," she called over the noise of their fellow shoppers.

At a row of dolls, Evan faced the stroller forward so Lily could see. "Do you like any of these?" he asked her, kneeling beside her.

Instead of looking at the dolls, Lily studied his face, then reached for it. She patted his stubbled cheek.

He let her examine his face, his Adam's apple working. There was a suspicious shininess to his eyes.

Vanessa's throat felt a little tight, seeing them get to know one another. Tactfully, she turned away and selected a couple of simple baby dolls. After she'd given father and daughter a moment, she turned back and held both dolls out to Lily. "We'll see which one she reaches for," she told Evan.

Lily chose a doll with molded plastic hair and pale green pajamas. "It comes with a bottle and a blanket. It's perfect." Vanessa tried to take the box from Lily, then gave up and let her hold it. "I forgot to ask if there's a cost limit," she said to Evan ruefully.

"No, but I think I've reached my shopping limit," he said. "This is overwhelming."

"You do look a little…glazed. Come on, let's check out."

After a long, hot wait in line, during which Lily joined in a chorus of crying babies, they made it outside. The baby seemed miserable in her stroller, reaching out for them, so Vanessa plucked her out and carried her up and down the block while Evan put their purchases in the back of his car.

"Next is clothes," she told him when he returned.

His forehead wrinkled. "Um...okay."

"Do you want to drive out to the big box stores on the highway? Everything will be cheaper, but it'll be super crowded with all the Black Friday bargain hunters."

"Let's just get the basics here in town," he said.

"Then we'll go to Katie's Kids' Klothes, up the street. It'll be good to support a local business."

"Sure." He let out a barely perceptible sigh.

"And then we'll get hot chocolate and pick up Declan and go home," she promised. She was enjoying the crowds and the excitement, but it wasn't for everyone. Including Evan, which wasn't all that surprising. He was a little on the introverted side.

The street was crowded, and when someone called Evan's name, she waved him off to see his friend and sat on a bench. Lily felt heavy in her arms, her eyes drooping. Snickers flopped down on the ground beside her.

She was aware of a warm, happy feeling in her chest, one that shouldn't be there.

Today was about being a professional nanny for Evan, working to earn the hefty paycheck he was offering. But so far, their shopping trip had felt anything but professional. Walking through the crowded store with Evan, managing Lily's mood, discussing which items would be best for the baby...all of it had felt more like the family she'd never had.

When she was a kid, Christmas holidays had been a fraught time, both before and after their father's death. In her twenties, the season had involved partying and restricted eating and loneliness.

There had been some good holiday times with Luke and Declan. And there'd been that one wonderful Christmas with Evan and Gramma Vi. But none of it had been the stuff of romantic TV movies, and on some level, she'd always longed for that.

Holidays were emotional already, and when you added in Evan and his adorable baby, her own feelings were, of course, heightened. She'd loved their time together before, too much. She'd known it couldn't last and she'd curtailed it. That was why Evan was guarded with her; she'd hurt him, badly.

Activities like they were doing now were making it both better and worse. She was making it up to him in a sense, helping him with the problem of caring for Lily. But she was also making it worse.

He was still having some kind of feelings for her. What kind, she couldn't tell.

She knew her own feelings, though. She was longing for something she'd always wanted and never had, and pinning that longing onto Evan. That moment when Lily had reached up and touched his face and he'd gotten teary... Oh, her heart.

The problem was, getting all tangled up with feelings for Evan Dukas would be a disaster for her. High, high stress. Whether he rejected her or embraced her, she'd pay a price.

Her psyche was weak. She had to do everything she could to protect herself, lest she go over the edge again.

She wanted, desperately, to be a good mother. To give Declan the simple, loving childhood he deserved.

That meant she needed to keep a distance from Evan. She needed to stay out of family-like situations. Do more on her own, to practice being strong.

Apparently sensing her turmoil, Snickers pushed himself up and leaned against her legs.

When Evan came back, she stood. "I have an idea," she said. "Since Lily's tired and you're not much of a shopper, why don't you take her home? I'll pick out some clothes to get her through the next few days. If they don't fit, there's a good return policy, I'm sure."

He shook his head. "No. For one thing, we only have my car here. And for another, I need to learn how to shop for her. I need to learn everything, and fast. So let's go shopping for toddler clothes."

Vanessa blew out a sigh. He did have a point, but it was messing with her plan of de-escalating their connection. Messing with her heart. "Okay," she said. "You're the boss. Come on, Lily, let's go with Daddy."

So much for practicing strength and independence on her own. It looked like she was spending the rest of the day with Lily and Evan.

Evan straightened his spine as they walked into the baby clothing store. He'd gotten through some pretty hairy situations in his work on-site in Saudi Arabia. He could handle a day of shopping.

He hoped so, anyway.

Vanessa went immediately to a rack full of little-girl dresses and started looking through them. "Look how sweet," she said, holding up a red one trimmed with white fur. "She'd look like a little Mrs. Claus in it."

"She would." Evan tried to participate. "Is it her size?"

"Let's hold it up to her."

He held the baby out, his arms straight, hands under her armpits, and Vanessa held up the dress. He jiggled her a little to keep her happy, and she chortled.

"No. Too big, I think." She explained baby sizing as she flipped through the rest of the rack. "These are cute, but since she's so short of clothes, we should probably focus on basics."

"Hi, Vanessa!" A woman he didn't know approached and joined Vanessa. "Oh, my, those are adorable. Look at the elf costume!"

Women made no sense to Evan. He made a slow spin with Lily, showing her the sights of the shop. At least this place wasn't as crowded as the toy store had been.

Vanessa glanced over at him and seemed to consider whether to introduce him to her friend. They were far enough apart that she didn't have to acknowledge she was with him. Understandable if she didn't want to. He'd let it go either way.

She chose in his favor. She took a few steps toward him, holding her friend's arm. "Gabby, this is Evan Dukas. He's Gramma Vi's grandson, and he's going to be staying here in Chesapeake Corners for a while."

"It's nice to meet you, and I'm sorry to hear about your grandma's fall," the woman said. "Is she doing okay?"

"I think so," Evan said. Did everyone in town know about Gramma's health? "She's already getting in trouble with her nurses."

Gabby smiled. "That's a good sign. Please give her my best. And who's this little lady?"

He smiled down at Lily, secure in the crook of his arm. "This is my daughter, Lily."

"Hi, Lily," Gabby said in a slightly singsong voice.

Lily laughed. She put out her hand and waved.

Evan felt a surge of pride to see his daughter actually communicating. She was going to have a great personality, he could tell already.

"Awww, she's so cute! It's nice to meet you." Gabby turned to include Vanessa in the conversation. "I just came in to say hello. I'd better get back out to Noah and Sloane. We came downtown to see the shop windows, but Sloane wants to go in the toy store. That requires all hands on deck."

Vanessa and Gabby hugged.

"Bye, Snickers. Bye-bye, Lily," Gabby said, waving.

"Ba-ba," Lily said, waving.

As Gabby walked off, Evan turned to Vanessa. "She talked!"

Vanessa smiled. "She did. And she waved. Those are both signs of development. Speaking of," she said, "I called our family doctor, and she gave me the name of some pediatricians who specialize in development. There's one farther up the shore, and one in Baltimore."

"Thank you!" He was impressed and touched. "How'd you manage that on a holiday?"

Vanessa smiled. "My doctor's a workaholic, and we're kind of friends. I figured she'd be in her office early this morning, so I called and she answered her own phone."

"I appreciate it." He met her eyes and found it hard to look away.

Apparently, she did, too.

Evan drew in a breath as he remembered this feeling: of looking into Vanessa's eyes and seeing deep into her heart, a vulnerable heart, a good heart.

She looked away first, and Evan came out of his trance and reminded himself it *wasn't* a good heart. It was a betraying heart this woman had, and he needed to avoid getting caught up in some imagined connection with her.

"Um, let's go look at warm shirts and overalls," she said. Her voice sounded a little choked. Snickers nudged his nose into her hand.

"Right. Where are they?"

She pointed, and they headed back there and selected

clothes for Lily quickly and efficiently. It was as if that moment of bonding had never happened.

Only it *had* happened.

He'd never have expected he could feel *that* again, and so quickly, with Vanessa. Whenever he'd thought of her in the past few years, it had been with distaste. Well, maybe not distaste. In his lonelier moments, as his marriage had failed and ended, he might have lingered on a pleasant memory or two: walking arm in arm with Vanessa, feeling understood and appreciated, touching her soft, shiny hair. But those pleasant emotions had dissipated when he'd thought about how abruptly it had all come to an end.

He needed to keep that end in mind, especially now that they were together. It wouldn't be easy to stay cold when holiday coziness and cheer were all around them, and when they were both focused on Lily.

But his priorities had changed in the past week, when he'd learned he was a father. Now more than ever, he needed to steer clear of any emotional entanglement that might end in harm to his daughter.

He couldn't steer clear of Vanessa, but he could keep his heart closed to her. No matter how hard, that was exactly what he needed to do.

Chapter Five

Vanessa had hoped to pick up Declan from her brother's quickly and get home.

Get away from Evan. Although that wasn't entirely possible since she was Lily's temporary nanny. But after that moment, or whatever it was, in the clothing store, Evan had told her curtly that she should take the rest of the evening off, that he didn't want to monopolize her time, that she only needed to care for Lily for the morning on Saturday. He'd fallen all over himself trying to put distance between them.

It was a little hurtful. Vanessa liked attention and admiration as well as the next woman.

Mostly, though, she'd been glad of it. She didn't need the stress of getting attracted to Evan, and the clean, wholesome lifestyle he represented, all over again. She'd just have to pull away from him in the end, and if last time were any indication, it would be devastating.

But when they'd shown up at her brother's house, Luke had Declan up on a ladder, showing him how to string Christmas lights on the tall bushes around the front door. Angie had tugged them aside and asked them to stay for dinner. She and Luke were worried about their foster kids, who were spending this holiday time with their birth family. They needed company and a distraction.

What could Vanessa say but okay? Evan had frowned, but when they'd gone inside and he'd smelled Angie's lasagna, he'd caved.

The meal and companionship had eased the tension between Vanessa and Evan. Lily was adorable, and Angie had held and fed her. Declan told them all about the amazing day he'd had helping his uncle. Snickers lay on the floor beside Angie's sweet Cavalier King Charles spaniel, Peppy. It was fun, festive, relaxing.

Vanessa and Angie cleaned up while Luke, Evan and Declan brought down Christmas decorations from the attic, taking turns entertaining Lily between loads.

"Thanks for the meal," Vanessa said to Angie as she ran a sink full of soapy water. "It was so good. Declan loves lasagna, and it looks like Evan does, too."

"You tucked in a fair amount yourself," Angie said, and then clapped a hand to her mouth. "I'm sorry. I don't want to trigger you by talking about food and what you eat."

"It's fine. I'm fine. I loved the meal, too." Truthfully, she'd been surprised by her own appetite. While it had been just her and Evan and Lily, she'd felt a little sick to her stomach. Once they'd all talked and laughed together, though, she'd forgotten her stomachache and enjoyed the meal.

She brought in dishes from the table while Angie washed pans and put the dishes in the dishwasher. They worked together companionably, which in itself was an amazing and wonderful thing. At one point, they'd been terribly at odds and Angie had pretty much hated Vanessa. But they'd worked through it, and now they were good friends.

"I appreciate you guys staying," Angie said now. "I'm trying not to focus on the kids and how they're doing, but it's scary to love them so much and yet not have control."

"I didn't think their biological parents were opposing the adoption," Vanessa said.

"They don't, or they say they don't. But if they get their acts together and spend time with the kids, who knows? Right now, the kids' grandparents are supervising the visit. What if they decide that together, they can all manage custody?"

"That must be so hard." Vanessa rested a hand on Angie's back for a moment.

"It is." Angie wiped beneath her eye with the back of her hand. "But it was great to have Declan with us today, and then to meet Evan and have you guys here for dinner."

"It's good for Declan to spend time with you guys," Vanessa said. "He feels a little displaced by your foster kids, to be honest. He's always been so close to Luke. And Luke's a great influence."

"What about Evan?" Angie asked slyly. They'd explained at dinner how Vanessa was staying in Gramma Vi's place and working as a temporary nanny for Lily. "He could be an additional male role model for Declan. He seems really nice."

A burst of male laughter sounded from the living room, followed by Lily's signature chortle.

Evan. Vanessa thought again about that moment in the shop, looking into his eyes.

"Well?" Angie plunged an empty salad bowl into her sink full of soapy water. "Evan's nice, isn't he?"

"He… Yes, he is. But…" She trailed off, took the rinsed bowl from Angie and dried it. "Where does this go?"

"Top shelf." Angie pointed. "What's the tea between you and Evan?"

"There's no tea."

Angie raised a skeptical eyebrow.

"Or if there is," Vanessa said, "there shouldn't be. That's all over with."

"You knew him before?"

Vanessa sucked in a breath and let it out in a sigh. "Yes. Briefly. We had a little thing one holiday season a while back."

"Before...before Declan?" That topic was dancing on the edge of the issues between them.

"Yes. Before Declan. But I can't go back there, and I'm sure he doesn't want to, anyway."

"Are you sure? There's a certain spark between the two of you."

"There better not be. Sparks are stressful."

Angie laughed. "They are, but in a good way."

"Not for me." Vanessa wiped the counter. "I'm not strong like you. I need to keep my stress level low so I can be a good mom to Declan."

"And Evan is stressful?"

"Evan is stressful."

Angie looked thoughtful as she let the water out of the sink. "You say you're not strong, but I disagree. You're stronger than you realize. Look at all you've accomplished."

"I've accomplished nothing compared to you. Or compared to Luke, or to most people."

Angie shook her head. "We all have different stories. You've worked so hard to overcome your eating disorder, and you're doing great. You've been a huge blessing to Gramma Vi. She raves about you all the time."

That made Vanessa smile. "I've been blessed to work for her." She wished it could go on forever, but the truth was, Gramma Vi was unlikely to stay in her house much longer, if she returned there at all.

The thought of the older woman growing weaker and

needing more care than Vanessa could provide tightened her throat. They'd gotten so close.

Angie got a broom and dustpan and swept under the table, collecting the few crumbs Snickers had missed. "The main thing is, though, that you're a great mom to Declan. You've really come through for him."

"He's my why."

"He's a great kid, and that's all you," Angie said kindly.

Soon they went into the front room to admire the wall full of boxes the men had brought downstairs for decorating. Angie went right to Lily and picked her up, swaying with her, looking wistful.

It was sweet. Vanessa knew that Angie had desperately wanted kids, but life circumstances hadn't permitted her to have them. Now she was thriving as a wife and a foster mom, but there was still a little bit of baby hunger in her eyes.

Vanessa tried to avoid looking at Evan. Then he and Luke moved a big box, and she couldn't help watching.

"Two good-looking men," Angie said, winking at her.

Vanessa couldn't deny it. But when she caught Evan's eye, he looked quickly away.

As they stood doing the usual predeparture chatting, Vanessa leaned into her brother's shoulder. He put an arm around her and squeezed. "You're doing great," he said. "And so's Declan. He was a big help today."

"Thank you for having him here. He loves doing things with you."

Angie was chatting with Evan, talking about people they might know in common. "I think I remember your first husband," Evan said to Angie. "Weren't the two of you at a fundraiser for Opera Philadelphia a few years back?"

Luke caught Evan's eye and held up a hand, stopping that

line of conversation. He nodded sideways at Declan, who was playing with Lily on the floor.

"Sure," Evan said quickly. "I get it."

He got *what*? Vanessa felt the lasagna in her stomach curdle. Did he think Oscar wasn't a topic to discuss in front of a child, any child, or did he guess at the real connection between Declan and Oscar?

But she doubted he'd guessed. Because Evan, moral, straitlaced Evan, wouldn't continue talking and laughing if he knew the whole sordid story.

Snickers whined and nudged his nose into her hand. She knelt to pet him, and then, as the others continued to talk, she sank down onto the floor. Immediately, Snickers pushed his way into her lap. He was too big to be a lap dog, but he was trained to do deep pressure therapy when he sensed extreme anxiety in his owner.

Apparently, he was sensing that now, and no wonder. Vanessa felt like a million tiny hummingbirds were flying, trapped, inside her chest.

She'd thought she was over the shame of her past actions. She'd worked hard in therapy, and prayed hard, gotten herself together. She even felt good about herself, sometimes.

As they gathered coats and hats and walked outside, Vanessa's stomach continued to churn.

She'd hoped the family dinner would ease the stress she felt around Evan, and it had started out that way.

Now, though, thinking about her past and wondering if Evan would find out about it, she felt more stressed out than ever.

Evan avoided Vanessa as much as he could throughout the rest of the weekend.

It made for awkward times at home. Declan was friendly,

and the dog was adorable, and Lily was starting to want to be around Vanessa. Trying to separate from the one-big-happy-family vibe didn't really work.

Moreover, it seemed to make him more obsessed with Vanessa than ever.

He was so distressed about it that he mentioned it to his grandmother when he visited her at the hospital.

"I don't want to be involved with her," he said, "but it's tough to stay apart when she's Lily's nanny and living in the same house."

"Why be apart?" she said. "There are other options in between cold and hot. You can never have too many friends. Why not look at her as a friend?"

He examined the idea from every direction and couldn't find a flaw in it. His gramma was a wise woman.

So that was what he'd do: look at Vanessa as a friend.

When he arrived home from the hospital, a very nostalgic sight and smell greeted him. Vanessa and Declan sat at the kitchen table, eating grilled cheese and tomato soup. Lily was in her booster seat, eating bits of grilled cheese sandwich. The dog lay at Lily's feet, alert. Even as he walked in, a piece of sandwich fell to the floor, to be neatly grabbed and consumed by Snickers.

"How's Gramma Vi?" Vanessa asked. She sounded guarded, wary.

And no wonder. He'd been confusing her with his coldness, no doubt.

"She's doing well," he said, sinking into a chair beside Lily.

"Ba-ba-DA-da-da!" she cried, reaching for him.

"Aww, she missed you, Dad," Vanessa said.

His heart melted with love. He pulled her out of the booster seat and onto his lap. She arched back, reaching for the sandwich pieces. Hastily, he grabbed a couple and let her take them from his hand.

"When's Gramma Vi coming home?" Declan asked.

"Well...she has to go to the rehab center first," he explained. "She needs a lot of physical therapy. But if all goes well, she can come visit as early as next weekend."

"Nice." Vanessa stood and started clearing plates. "Would you like a sandwich before I clean up?" she asked, in the polite tone you'd use for a guest. "It's quick to make."

"No, that's okay." He'd better start the friendship thing now, before he ruined any chance of it happening. The idea of going forward with this kind of awkwardness for a whole month made him miserable.

He walked over to the bag he'd brought in, Lily perched on his hip. "I was wondering if you all would like to watch a movie," he said. He produced a giant bag of popcorn. "Gramma told me where she keeps her Christmas movies. She said she doesn't have a streaming service, but that her DVD player works fine."

"It does," Declan said.

Vanessa's brow wrinkled. It looked like she didn't want to participate. Which was her right, but it disappointed him. Why that was, he didn't want to examine too closely.

"It sounds like fun, but the baby can't eat popcorn," she told him. "It's a choking hazard."

"More for me," Declan said, bouncing up from the table. He came over to Lily, held up her hand and gave her a gentle high five.

He was a good kid, Declan. Evan was really starting to like him.

"No big deal," Vanessa said. "Lily can eat corn puffs. I picked some up from the grocery store." She went to a cupboard and pulled out a cylinder of food.

"You shouldn't be spending your money. Keep a record and I'll reimburse you. We'll have to figure out a system."

She waved a hand. "We'll work it out."

He liked that about her. She probably had a tenth of the money he did, but she wasn't sweating the details like some of his wealthier friends did, using their phone calculators to divide up the bill at restaurant dinners. Her attitude made him want even more than usual to be fair about money.

She cleaned up while he got Lily bathed and changed, and they met in the living room half an hour later. Declan was still upstairs taking his shower.

Vanessa turned to him. "Why the turnaround?" she asked.

"What do you mean?" he hedged. He hadn't expected her to confront him about it.

She waved a hand from the TV screen to the bowl of popcorn. "This is cozy, but you've been avoiding me all weekend. So, I'm surprised."

He nodded. Upstairs, he heard the shower turn off.

He wasn't good at pretty words or hiding the truth. He'd be honest, and fast. "We talked about how it would be good to maintain some professional distance," he said. "It didn't seem to work too well, for me, anyway. It felt awkward, and I don't want to go through the holiday season that way. So I was thinking we could try being...friends."

"Friends?" She raised an eyebrow.

He nodded. "Friends for the holidays." And then, since she looked skeptical and he really, really wanted this to work, he reached for more ammunition. "For us to be friends is best for the children."

"Well..." Her forehead wrinkled. She was thinking about it. Then, she nodded. "I guess it's worth a try." She held out a hand, and he shook hers.

He noticed every nuance of her touch. A strong grip. Soft

skin, except that he could feel a few calluses. She did a lot of housework and yard work, keeping up this old place. Her nails were short and unpolished.

She seemed to have no reaction to his touch. She just pulled her hand back briskly and smiled.

That was good. This could be managed.

Declan came down in a ripped but clean-looking T-shirt and flannels. He dived for the recliner. "I call the big chair!"

"Okay with me," Evan said. "I'm sitting by the popcorn." He held out the large bowl into which Vanessa had poured a generous amount of the popcorn he'd brought.

Snickers lay at Vanessa's feet, his bright, alert eyes following every move of the popcorn bowl.

"No fair!" Declan jumped out of the chair and came dancing over in pretend ninja fashion.

Lily laughed, her eyes following him. Declan was fun for her. Lively. She seemed to be developing a case of hero worship.

"Declan! If you spill that popcorn you're cleaning it up." Vanessa sounded just slightly stern. "Go in the kitchen and get your own bowl. Use the red one."

Declan ninja'd his way into the kitchen and soon returned with not only a big red bowl of popcorn, but also a plastic container of cookies. He opened it up and held it out to Evan. Chocolate chip, homemade. He took three.

They'd chosen a funny movie about a family going home for the holidays and struggling to get there. It was a good choice, colorful for Lily, who was starting to doze in Evan's arms, and funny for the rest of them.

Evan had put logs and kindling in the fireplace earlier, such that it only took a match to get it going. Soon the room was warm, fragrant with popcorn and cookies, and ringing with the sound of their laughter. Lily fell asleep, curled up between Evan and the arm of the couch. Vanessa moved the popcorn bowl closer to Evan so he wouldn't have to disturb her by reaching.

He was glad to see that Vanessa took the occasional handful to eat, herself. As far as he could tell, she mostly ate normally—light, nowhere near as much as he and Declan ate, but that could just be because she was so petite. It didn't take much food to keep her going.

During a particularly funny scene, he looked over to see her unguardedly laughing, her head thrown back, her throat long and white, blond hair settling around her shoulders.

He looked down. Yes, Lily was asleep.

The urge he felt was impossible to resist. Carefully, he moved closer.

She laughed again. "Did you see that, Declan?"

No answer. Just a soft snore.

"He's asleep," she concluded, and turned to Evan. "Did you see it?"

He nodded. He was laughing, too, but more at her enthusiasm than at the movie. He'd lost track of the plot.

His whole body seemed to tug toward her, the yearning way more intense than when they'd watched movies with Gramma twelve years ago.

Of course it was more intense. They were older and they'd both been married. They knew what kind of closeness they were yearning for.

At least, he did, and he hadn't back then. Vanessa had been his first serious girlfriend. It had felt serious to him, anyway, despite the brevity of their connection.

She probably hadn't taken it seriously. He'd heard later that he was one in a long line of men she'd dated.

He wanted to ask her why she'd left. Why, when he'd asked if she'd visit him in Boston, she'd put her hands on her hips and told him life wasn't a Christmas movie. That they'd had a fun time, sure, but she wasn't going to see him again.

He'd been naive back then. He hadn't given any thought to what it would mean to fall for her. He'd just done it, acting on impulse.

He looked at her. She'd leaned her head back against the couch, and she wasn't watching the movie. She was watching him. They were inches apart. Both of them breathing quickly.

The fire crackled, and the laugh track in the movie was just background noise. He could smell her perfume, the same citrusy smell she'd worn when they'd dated before.

He leaned a little closer, his thinking brain going into hibernation. His hand slid along the back of the couch to cup her neck and tangle in her hair.

He was going to kiss her. It was inevitable.

"Mom?" Declan said sleepily.

In a flash, they were apart. Evan cleared his throat and fussed with Lily's blanket, and Vanessa turned to her son, scooting toward him and leaning away from Evan.

Her cheeks were a telltale shade of pink.

It was a good thing, a very good thing, that Declan had woken up, that he'd spilled popcorn all over the recliner, that Snickers roused himself and came over to help clean up. It was good that Vanessa had to turn on the lights to see all the spillage.

The credits of the movie rolled.

Evan sucked in a breath and let it out slowly. Did it again.

And then he stood and forced a smile. "I'm going to put Lily to bed," he said. "And I think I'll read in my room. Can you lock up before you go upstairs?"

She nodded without looking at him.

Hmm. Their first attempt at this friendship thing had been a complete failure.

Chapter Six

The "let's be friends" idea was actually more stressful to Vanessa than being enemies at odds with one another would have been. During the week after that cozy, wonderful, disturbing family movie night, Vanessa scheduled a meeting with her old therapist and leaned on Snickers to get her through.

Evan had been about to kiss her. The way he'd looked at her, the way he'd cupped the back of her head, tangling his fingers in her hair... Yeah. There was no doubt.

What was really bad was that she had almost let him.

She was thankful that Declan had awakened when he did. So very thankful. If things felt uncomfortable between her and Evan now, she could only imagine how it would be if they'd given in to their instincts.

Kissing, and the aftermath of it, would have seriously raised the awkwardness level in the house.

She had the suspicion that Evan would have taken a kiss seriously, and what then? Vanessa knew she couldn't manage a relationship. She wasn't strong enough. She'd have had to push him away, again. The first time she'd done it, it had almost destroyed her. There could be no second time.

So she avoided him as much as was possible. When they had to interact over Lily's care, she tried to assume the persona of a cool, professional nanny. It helped, sort of, that he seemed to be of the same mind. Stay apart, back off, keep it cool.

Thursday night provided a good break. Vanessa was hosting a couple of friends for Bible study, and Evan offered to take Declan to his hockey clinic, eliminating the need for Vanessa to seek out a ride for him. Once they'd left, she heaved a sigh of relief and hummed as she arranged a spread of snacks and desserts on the table.

Snickers gave a sharp bark, and before Vanessa could get to the back kitchen door, her friends were letting themselves in.

Angie and Gabby hung their coats on hooks by the door and put their wet shoes and boots on the black rubber tray beneath. Their cheeks were rosy, and they were laughing at something that had happened in therapy dog training class. They were carrying their Bibles, and just seeing them lifted a weight off Vanessa's shoulders. With Angie and Gabby, she could be herself.

"There's that adorable baby," Angie cooed, bending close to Lily to pat her leg. Vanessa had found an old playpen in Gramma's attic. She'd set it up beside their table and plunked Lily in it with a couple of quiet toys.

"She stays in that?" Gabby asked. "How old is she?"

"She's eighteen months, aren't you, sweetie?" Vanessa planted a big, loud kiss on top of the baby's head, making her laugh. "And I know what you're going to ask next. No, she's not walking or even pulling up yet. Evan's going to take her to a developmental pediatrician next week."

"Ah." Gabby studied the child. "Looks like she's trying to pull up."

"I know. Isn't she cute?" Vanessa had clipped a couple of colorful stuffed toys to the playpen's rims, and periodically,

Lily reached for them, shifting around and tugging the sides of the playpen with her little hands.

"Where's Declan?" Angie asked.

Vanessa pulled out chairs and ushered the women to the kitchen table. "Evan took Declan to hockey practice."

"Oh, he did?" Gabby raised her eyebrows at Angie. "See, I told you."

"Told her what?" Vanessa frowned, then waved a hand. "Never mind. I don't think I want to know."

She could guess. Her friends, both newly and happily married, wanted to see her find someone to love.

But they didn't have the complications Vanessa had. Their relationships had added to their lives. Vanessa was afraid that a relationship would ruin hers, and Declan's, too.

Fortunately, Angie changed the subject. "Look how good Snickers is," she said, squatting down in front of the dog. Snickers sat upright, as still as a statue, only his eyes moving. "Okay if I pet him?"

"Yep. He's out of harness. Just hanging around."

"He doesn't get into the snacks? He's tall enough to reach the table."

"No, he's really a good boy." Vanessa stopped to rub his ears. "Not that I'd leave a package of steak out within his reach, but he mostly doesn't table-surf."

"Peppy's too short to reach the table, but she tries," Angie said.

"Caramel's really too short, unless Sloane gives her a lift. But she's getting a little too used to table scraps. I need to lay down the law." Gabby smiled, and Vanessa got the feeling that she was too happy and content to lay down a whole lot of laws.

Soon they were all settled around the table with cups of

hot tea and plates of snacks in front of them. "Let's dig in to our readings," Gabby said, always the teacher.

They'd been meeting for several months now, and they took a theme for each meeting. This month's theme was perfect for Vanessa: strength.

It was what she lacked. What she needed. What she longed for, so that she could be a good role model for her son.

"Did everyone find a few verses about our topic?" Angie asked.

"Yes. There are tons. Though we probably chose some of the same ones." Gabby started flipping through her Bible.

"Let's read them out loud," Angie suggested. So they did, and Vanessa let the rich, meaningful verses wash over her.

"What's your current need for strength?" Gabby asked.

"Kids," Angie said promptly. "Our three fosters came back from their family pretty wild. It's taken days for them to calm down. They're confused about where home really is."

"That's got to be hard." Vanessa squeezed Angie's hand. "What about you, Gabby?"

Gabby sighed. "Noah and I clashed over how to discipline Sloane this week. She's so much better, but she still needs a lot of structure. I think that means regular meals and bedtimes, and Noah thinks it means rules." Sloane, their daughter, had been diagnosed with oppositional defiant disorder a few years ago.

"Ugh. Parenting clashes. I never thought Luke and I would be fortunate enough to be parents. Now that we're fostering, though, we're having to face our differences."

"This is when it's easiest to be a single mom," Vanessa quipped, then looked anxiously at Angie. Her route to being a single mom had been complicated, and Angie's late husband had been involved.

Angie seemed to read her mind and patted her hand.

"Don't worry, you won't be single forever," she said. "You'll get into these kind of silly fights soon enough."

Vanessa shook her head. "I've got plenty on my plate with Declan and Snickers," she said.

"And Lily? And Evan?" Gabby teased.

"Definitely not. Well, Lily's fine." She looked down at the playpen. Lily had curled up on the bottom of it, sucking her thumb. "Uh-oh. I'd better put her down before she gets too deeply asleep."

When she returned, the other two looked up with similar guilty expressions. "Yes, we've been talking about you," Angie admitted. "We worry."

"I'm fine," Vanessa said, waving a hand. "I'm doing well, actually." Was it true? She mostly felt it to be. She looked from one friend to the other and couldn't hide the truth. "Actually, I've been better. Having Gramma Vi in rehab, and having Evan and Lily here, well... Yeah. It's not easy."

"Be strong and courageous," Gabby said. "That's my favorite of all the verses we read. From Joshua, right?"

Vanessa nodded. It was a verse she'd been drawn to lately. "Joshua 1:9," she said.

"My question is, how exactly do we do that? How do we make ourselves strong and courageous?"

"Not on your own," Angie said. "From your connection to God. 'They that wait upon the Lord shall renew their strength.'"

"Right," Gabby said. "'The joy of the Lord is your strength.' Which I take to mean, focus on rejoicing in our faith, and strength will come."

"Let's pray for that, then," Angie said, and they did. And Vanessa felt a little better.

Until she heard a car door slam outside. Declan came

stomping into the house, tossing hockey gear in a haphazard heap by the table, not greeting anyone.

"Declan!" Vanessa said. "What's wrong?"

But he was already stomping upstairs.

"Looks like you'll need all the strength you can get," Gabby said quietly as Evan came in the door.

Vanessa waved at him and went to the foot of the stairs. "Declan. Come back down as soon as you've washed up, please."

"Let him go," Evan said. "I already spoke with him."

Vanessa felt her eyebrows shoot up into her hairline. Really, he was telling her how to manage her kid?

"Sorry to disturb the discussion, ladies," Evan said breezily. "I'll just head for my room."

"Oh, we're done, anyway," Angie said, standing.

"Yes. I have to get home." Gabby looked at the clock. Both women started gathering their purses and Bibles.

Vanessa turned toward Evan. "What happened?"

"He took an attitude with another boy. I told him to cut it out, and he called me a few choice names."

"What?" That didn't sound like Declan. "I'm sorry. I'll speak to him."

"I already did."

Heat rose to her face. "Excuse me, but I'm his mother. I'll do the discipline around here."

A throat cleared from the other side of the room. Gabby and Angie were putting on their coats, and she walked over to see them out.

"Be strong and courageous," Gabby murmured.

"Parenting together is hard," Angie added.

"We're not…"

But before she could finish the sentence, they were out the door.

Right. Strong and courageous. She took a deep breath as she watched her friends through the window, making sure they got to their cars.

Snickers came over and leaned against her, and she reached down and rubbed his floppy ears, taking comfort in his presence. Snickers was on her side, at least.

And God. Great, just great. Right after Bible study, she was relying on her dog?

She glanced upward. "Help me lean on You, Lord," she prayed. "Help me rejoice in You. Give me strength."

She turned back toward Evan, but he was already headed into his suite, his heavy steps sounding a lot like Declan's stomps.

Great. Now she had two cranky men in the house.

She appreciated the Bible study, and she appreciated Evan taking Declan to practice. But if letting Evan do her that kind of favor added to her stress, that was all the more reason to limit things.

She started clearing the table, slowly. There had been times when she'd longed for an involved man in her life, especially as Declan grew. Her brother, Luke, had been a rock in that regard, but he had his own family to care for now.

Evan was here, and Declan was bound to look at him as some kind of male authority figure, with all the pluses and minuses that contained.

Did she keep Declan away from Evan? Tell Evan he couldn't discipline Declan, or even be involved with him at all?

She didn't want Declan to be devoid of male role models. But she also didn't want him to be devoid of a mother if she went back into her stress.

She was going to have to talk to Evan about it, unfortunately.

* * *

Evan half expected the knock on his bedroom door that came half an hour after Vanessa had shut him down. She must be feeling bad, ready to apologize.

She'd never ventured into his suite of rooms before. Although she was in and out of Lily's room, next door to his suite, on a regular basis, she'd always avoided even glancing in on the frequent occasions when he had the door between his room and Lily's open.

Hastily, he threw a pair of dirty socks into his laundry basket and then went to the door.

She was standing there, one hand on her hip, Snickers beside her, panting. Her expression was anything but conciliatory.

"You didn't answer your phone," she said now.

"I use the do-not-disturb function at night." Only Gramma's number, and her rehab center, could get through. He held the door wider. "It's not a problem. You can come in."

She did, and then stood looking uncomfortable. It was as if she were trying not to look around. Trying *not* to interact with him any more than possible.

Was the fact that this was his bedroom making her uncomfortable? "Have a seat," he said, gesturing to the easy chair that faced away from his bed. He sat on the love seat. "What's up?"

She settled into the chair, and Snickers flopped down beside her. Then she met his eyes evenly. "I didn't like the idea of you disciplining Declan," she said. "That's my job."

He blinked. So, definitely not an apology, then. "Really? You're still upset about that?"

She flushed. "Yes. I am. Did you expect something different?"

Irritation flashed through him. He'd taken time he didn't

have to drive her son to practice and then manage an uncomfortable series of events. And she was criticizing him for it? "I thought you were coming in here to apologize," he said.

"No. You didn't respond to what I said before. I didn't know if you heard me."

"Oh, I heard you." He took a deep breath, trying to calm his annoyance. "Do you want to hear what happened? Or would you rather just rush to judgment?"

"I didn't—" She cut off. Paused. Took a deep breath, just like he had. "Okay. What happened?"

He noticed she'd gone stiff, as if she were bracing herself. Snickers sat up and leaned against her leg, and she lay a hand atop his shaggy head.

Suddenly, he wasn't sure he wanted to tell her.

"What did Declan do?" she prodded.

Well, Evan had started this. He probably had to carry it through to completion now. "A kid said something to Declan that made him mad."

"What was it?"

"I'm not entirely sure," he said. "Something about his father."

"Ohhhh." She deflated visibly, shoulders slumping, looking down at the floor. Then she lifted her head and met his eyes. "How did Declan respond?" she asked quietly.

"He got mad. Got in the kid's face and kind of loomed over him. Started talking about how *his* father didn't even have a job but just sat around at home."

"Oh, no," she said, her forehead wrinkling. "Do you happen to know which child it was?"

"I don't know his name," he said. "Little guy, a redhead. I made Declan apologize to the child. Then I watched while his parents called him over to see what was going on. His dad seems to be in a wheelchair."

"Oh, no." She blew out a breath. "It must have been Hunter Bradenton. I can't believe Declan lashed out with a comment like that about a disabled veteran. I hope Hunter won't share Declan's comment with his dad, but he probably will."

"Exactly," he said. "I didn't think that behavior should go unpunished. I told Declan that we were going home as soon as practice was over. I didn't let him stay for pizza with the rest of the team." He'd felt proud of himself, actually. The punishment had seemed about right for the crime.

She frowned. "I still think I should be the only one who corrects him," she said. "I'm grateful that you took him to practice, and I'm sorry you had to deal with all of that. But you don't know the whole story. Declan is…sensitive. About his father."

Evan had started to get an inkling of that tonight. "Declan was pretty mad at me," he said. "He said something about how I wasn't his father. Called me a name, and said his dad was richer than me and if he were still alive, he'd punch me."

She closed her eyes and shook her head, slowly. "I'm sorry he called you a name, and I *will* give him a consequence for that. He knows better."

Evan would have given a lot to know the story of Declan's father, but she didn't volunteer even a tidbit. "I still wish you'd left the discipline to me," she said.

She was like a terrier worrying at a bone. He frowned, irritated. "Are his teachers allowed to correct his behavior?"

"Of course. But—"

"His coaches?"

"Yes. But you're neither one of those."

"True," he said, "but think about it. You're taking care of my child. Making decisions about her. Teaching her a little right and wrong already, aren't you?"

"I guess." She sighed, rested her elbow on the arm of the

chair and propped her cheek on it. "I don't know. I didn't have good role models of parents, and it shows in a situation like this. You probably did the right thing. I'm sorry I doubted you."

He smiled then, her apology restoring his good mood. "We're all learning as we go along," he said. "You know way more than I do about parenting. So don't beat yourself up."

"Yeah. I should get to bed. Let you do the same." She rose from her chair, and Snickers stood, too, and stretched, then shook himself. "Thanks again," Vanessa said. "I'm sorry for my overreaction."

He stood and, without conscious intent, pulled her into a hug. "You're a great mom," he said.

She clung to him for just a millisecond, letting her face rest against his chest.

Warmth flashed through him. He could stay like this forever.

She stepped back, and he let go of her instantly, sternly telling himself that this was just friendship, that was all it could be.

As she left, not looking at him, her cheeks pink, as he closed the door after her, he felt the most immense longing in his chest.

What would it be like to have someone with whom to share parenting responsibilities? Someone to hold like that when times were hard for either of them?

Women aren't reliable. You can't count on them. He'd learned it from Vanessa, and his wife's actions had solidified the idea. *Women aren't reliable*, he reminded himself again.

This time, the mantra rang hollow in his own head, leaving him empty inside.

Evan felt tender toward Vanessa after their late-night talk. Too tender. At risk of making dangerous mistakes.

Except he was having a hard time thinking of her as a danger, to him or to Lily. She did what she did for a reason.

Fortunately for his heart, they both got busy over the next few days. Work emergencies with his team kept Evan busy all day Friday, meaning that Vanessa had an extended day of caring for Lily. Saturday, they split Lily duties so they could each visit Gramma at the rehab facility, which didn't allow visits from young children.

Sunday, encouraged by him, Vanessa took the day off from Lily. She and Declan went to church in the morning and didn't come back until late in the day, apparently participating in a holiday market and craft workshop.

He was curious about how she'd resolved things with her son, but he didn't want to intrude. It just wasn't his business.

He kept reminding himself of that.

Monday meant a whole day together, and he also had to keep reminding himself that he shouldn't look forward to that quite so much as he was. The visit to the developmental pediatrician was serious business, Lily business. It was important enough that he wanted Vanessa to go with him, and she'd agreed. But there would be no time for things to get all warm and romantic. That was a good thing. Really, it was.

They left early to make the two-hour trip to Baltimore, and while he drove, Vanessa tried to keep Lily entertained. They'd hoped the baby would sleep on the way, so that she could be rested for her appointment. But Lily wasn't having it; she was talkative and wiggly and fussy by turns.

When they arrived in the upscale office, Evan's nerves got the best of him. He held Lily and paced. Up until now, he'd mostly compartmentalized his worrisome thoughts, focusing on the day-to-day routines of parenting and remote work. Now, though, they'd get some answers, and he couldn't seem to calm himself down.

What if there were something really wrong with Lily? What if she'd been so neglected that her little brain, or her body, was irreparably broken?

Fortunately, Dr. Hershel didn't keep them waiting. She greeted them professionally and took them to a large carpeted room that was more like a residential living room than an office. She encouraged them both to sit down. And she made it clear that she was in charge.

The pace of it was fast. The doctor had Lily eat a snack and drink from a sippy cup. She listened to Lily's babble and made notes. She held up toys and then hid them, testing whether Lily could figure out to crawl behind a screen to get them.

Evan's nerves felt as tight as a hydraulic clamp. Everything in him wanted to help Lily find the hidden toy, but when he started to stand to direct her, the doctor held up a hand. "She's not failing a test, Mr. Dukas," she said. "I'm just gathering information."

Last of all, the doctor addressed the physical issues that had initially gotten Vanessa's attention. She felt Lily's legs and arms, checking for strength and range of motion. When Lily started to fuss, she just smiled and continued, gentle but firm. "I save this part for last because they don't like it," she explained over Lily's increasingly loud cries.

Finally, she handed the baby off to them and moved to her computer. They took turns holding and comforting her while the doctor made notes.

A few minutes later, she beckoned both of them over to her desk. "It's good you caught what was going on," she said.

"Wasn't me," Evan hastened to clarify. "I know nothing about babies. Vanessa noticed and suggested this appointment."

Dr. H raised an eyebrow.

Embarrassed, Evan explained why he didn't know much about Lily's first eighteen months.

"I'm guessing there was neglect," she said. "Does that make sense given what you know of the mother?"

His fists clenched, and he consciously relaxed them. "It's possible," he said.

Vanessa jumped in. "Evan didn't know his wife was pregnant when she left," she explained. "He would never neglect his child." She looked over at him. "Isn't that right?"

"If I'd known of Lily's existence, I'd have taken over." Suddenly, he realized that Vanessa was trying to make sure he didn't get accused of child neglect. "Lily's mom will never have unsupervised visits as long as I can prevent it," he said.

The doctor studied him for a long moment. "Okay. All you can do is go forward from here." She made another note. "Early intervention will work wonders with Lily, I'm almost sure," she said. "This type of global delay is usually caused by a deficiency in care, but getting a baby into a better environment is more than 50 percent of the solution."

Evan's shoulders relaxed. "You think she'll be okay?"

The doctor held up a hand. "If you work at it," she said. "Pretty hard, right now. I'd like to get the early intervention folks out to do a formal assessment and start some therapy for her as soon as possible. They can come to your house, and it's free."

Evan was tapping notes into his phone.

"You can get her started with a few simple exercises," she said. She handed them a glossy pamphlet called "Helping Your Baby Catch Up." "Keep up with feeding her varied foods, like you've been doing. Her eating abilities are fine. Socially, she'll catch up quickly. She seems like a bright little girl."

Evan held on to those promising words as they finished the paperwork and left the office.

Lily fell asleep instantly on the drive back home, and Vanessa relaxed in the passenger seat beside Evan. They rode in comfortable silence for a while. It was a cold, crisp day, and the light dusting of snow on the ground just made everything brighter in the sun.

"Are you feeling okay about things?" she asked finally, looking over at him.

"I am," he said. "Thank you again for noticing the issue and helping to set up this appointment. I can't believe she's so far behind, but I'm hopeful she can catch up."

"I think she will. That doctor was a little abrupt, but she seems to know her stuff."

Evan hadn't even noticed her abruptness. "She's more like me, an engineering and science type," he said. "I kind of got her."

Vanessa laughed. "That's good. I won't be insulted on Lily's behalf, then."

After another couple of quiet minutes, Evan asked the question he'd been curious about. "Did you talk to Declan about that kid he argued with?"

"I did." She frowned. "I impressed on him that we don't hurt people back when they hurt us, because we don't know what they may be going through."

Her words stung. Evan knew he'd lashed out at Vanessa, in his mind at least, multiple times. She *had* hurt him, but he was starting to realize she must have been going through a lot, herself.

She went on, her voice musing. "That kid, his dad's issues are right there front and center, visible to everyone. Declan understands he was wrong, and he feels bad about it." She hesitated.

He could tell she had more to say. "Go on."

"It's awkward because...there are things about his father he's not ready to know yet."

I'm ready to know. "His dad wasn't involved in his life?" he asked cautiously.

"He was somewhat involved before he passed away, but... let's just say he had other priorities."

Evan frowned. "I resented my parents for having other priorities. I'm sure Declan isn't happy about it, either."

"You may be right." She reached for the radio knob and turned on music, loud enough that they couldn't talk.

Message received.

He didn't think he'd ever understand women. They could be strong and smart and understandable, like the pediatrician. But they could also be confusing, like Vanessa.

He needed to keep his eyes on the priority: Lily. Right now, Vanessa was good for her, and she'd be a major asset during this initial phase of helping Lily catch up developmentally. After that, it was anyone's guess. He had to balance Lily's immediate needs with the long-term risks of having a woman like Vanessa involved in Lily's—and his—life.

Chapter Seven

After the doctor visit, Vanessa managed the rest of the week well. She spent her days with Lily, doing the exercises suggested by the doctor, but also making sure the baby had rest and good food and plenty of playtime. In the evenings, Declan got involved. He encouraged Lily to bounce in her bouncy chair, helped her play with blocks, and made silly faces at her. Declan was a little guarded around Evan still, and Vanessa hadn't enlisted Evan for any help with him. Too much risk of conflict, and conflict was what she was trying to avoid.

When she and Evan had been driving home from the pediatrician, she'd felt terrifyingly tempted to reveal the story behind Declan's father. Thankfully, she had been able to avoid the temptation.

She'd been so lost back then. She hadn't grown up with religious faith or any concept that intimacy outside of marriage was wrong. She'd also been naive and needy, and it had led her to make a terrible mistake.

God had worked everything for good, giving her a wonderful child. But she couldn't expect Evan to understand any of it.

Evan seemed warm and kind sometimes, but he was a strongly moral man with a judgmental streak a mile wide.

She remembered that from their time together, and she had seen no evidence that he'd changed in that regard. If he knew the truth about her relationship with Declan's dad, he would hate her for it. Plain and simple.

Now that they were set up for the holidays, with her and Declan slated to stay in Gramma's place and Evan paying her a good salary for being Lily's caregiver, she wanted smooth sailing. No need to stir up the waters by telling him how stupid she'd been and what she'd done.

So she and Evan were cordial together, but not close like friends, not spending a lot of time together, all week.

Until Friday.

As they all got out of Evan's car at the Christmas tree farm—Evan, Vanessa, Declan, Lily and Snickers—Vanessa's stomach felt unsteady. This excursion had been all her idea. Was it a good one?

But one look at Declan's excited expression, and she knew it had been right to come.

Declan had arrived home from his early school dismissal in a bad mood. He'd refused to answer her questions, but she got the feeling he was still having some issues with other kids at school, stemming from the hockey practice incident. Even though she'd made him write a note of apology to the boy and his family, and she'd called the mother to check in and apologize herself, she couldn't fix everything. The parents had understood, but Declan had to learn to work out friend issues himself.

Lily had been extra fussy today, too. Possibly, she felt cooped up due to being in the house all day. As Vanessa had suspected right away, Lily seemed to be an extrovert who thrived on stimulation and people.

So when Vanessa had seen that the tree lot was having a one-day special on cutting your own Christmas trees, she'd approached Evan and suggested they go. He'd hesitated only briefly and then agreed.

Despite her qualms about spending this family-like time with Evan, she felt her shoulders relax as she breathed in the cold, pine-scented air. It was good for everyone, herself included, to get outside.

Evan was holding Lily, who looked adorable with her fur-lined snowsuit hood surrounding her chubby, pink-cheeked face. Declan ran ahead toward the trees. Snickers stayed at Vanessa's side, but the dog's alert eyes and panting smile suggested he wouldn't mind doing some running himself.

Evan and Vanessa spoke to an employee, who explained the protocol. Then they headed toward the neat, seemingly endless rows of evergreen trees. Evan pulled a flat, tray-like sled on which they could load the tree they cut down. Talk and laughter from other family groups sounded from both sides, but the farm was big enough, and the trees were planted thickly enough, that there was no one else in sight.

Declan zigzagged through the trees. "I like this one!" he said, pointing to the biggest tree in their area. Before either adult could respond, he was on to another. "Or this one!" He pointed to the fattest tree. Then he paused beside a tiny tree. "Or we could get a Charlie Brown tree, like this. If we don't have the money for the big ones."

Vanessa's heart squeezed. "We have our own Charlie Brown tree at home, remember? And we'll still put that one up somewhere. Maybe in the entryway." She'd bought the tabletop tree when Declan was small, and they'd used it every year, overloading it over time with ornaments Declan had made in school. Last year, she'd put it away decorated; it was that small.

"I measured Gramma's ceilings," Evan said. "They're

ten feet, so we can get a tree up to eight feet tall if we find one we like."

"How tall is that?" Declan asked doubtfully. He was still a little skittish around Evan after the hockey practice incident.

Evan walked over to a tall tree. "Let's see," he said. "I'm about six feet tall, and Lily is about three feet, two sitting down, so..." He lifted Lily and plunked her on his shoulders.

"Six plus two is eight. Cool!" Declan started looking at the taller trees.

Vanessa winced. "We don't have to get one that big," she said. "They're expensive, and I doubt we have enough lights or ornaments to cover such a big tree."

"Gramma has a ton of ornaments. And we can buy more lights. Let's let Declan pick out the tree."

Vanessa's heart melted a little. "Thank you, Evan," she said softly.

He smiled down at her. "You're welcome. Want to hold Lily?" He handed the baby off and then headed after Declan.

They spent a long time searching through the trees, mostly because Evan wanted to find a perfect one. Each time Declan got excited about a tree, Evan pointed out some flaw.

"Perfectionist," she teased him.

"I am, I admit it." He gave her a warm, crinkle-eyed smile.

They finally settled on a tall Scotch pine. Evan showed Declan how to use the saw lent to them by the tree farm, and Declan started to cut. He wasn't strong enough to do much—which Vanessa was happy about, because having him handle a saw was a little bit scary. Evan tactfully suggested they take turns, and Declan's movements became more sure as he modeled them on Evan.

"Tim-berrrrrr!" Declan and Evan shouted the word at the same time. They both jumped away. The tree crashed to the ground, and the two of them dragged it over onto the sled with the help of a roving employee. Talking and laughing together, they hauled the tree back to the central area, where a bonfire burned. People clustered around it, waiting while employees did a clean cut of the tree stumps and then helped to tie them onto cars.

While Evan managed that part, Vanessa sent Declan to get cups of hot chocolate and a cookie for Lily. When he returned, they sat on log benches around the fire.

A man in a wheelchair made his way over to them, revving it athletically over the frozen ground. He reached them and held out a hand to Vanessa. "I'm Hunter's father, Chuck Bradenton," he said. "Just wanted to say hello."

"It's nice to meet you in person," Vanessa said, her stomach lurching a little. She looked over at Declan.

His eyes widened. He wiped his hands along the sides of his jeans and glanced at Vanessa, then spoke. "I'm sorry I said a mean thing about you. I was mad at Hunter, but I was wrong to say what I did."

Vanessa's heart seemed to swell with pride. Declan had been wrong, done a bad thing, but this apology was unprompted by her and was clearly heartfelt. She hoped Hunter's father would see that and forgive Declan.

To her relief, the man waved a hand. "Hunter made a comment about your dad, too, from what I hear," he said. He turned and beckoned to his son, who was on the other side of the fire. "Hunter. Over here."

The boy came over, dragging his feet.

"Did you apologize to Declan yet, for what you said about his dad?"

Vanessa bit her lip. She wasn't sure this was the right way to go about reconciling the boys. More than that, she didn't want to discuss Declan's father in such a public setting, especially when Evan approached and stood behind her. A silent support, or a silent judge, she wasn't sure which.

"Sorry," Hunter muttered.

"It's okay. I'm sorry, too." Declan dug the frosty ground with the tip of his sneaker.

"Wanna go see the reindeers?" Hunter asked.

"They have *reindeer*?" Declan looked up at Vanessa. "Can I, Mom?"

"Sure. I'll come with you." She reached for her things.

Hunter's father spoke up. "It's okay, I can take them over." He gave Vanessa and Declan a slightly speculative look. "If that's okay with you."

Vanessa got the feeling that he wanted to see whether Vanessa would accept his supervision of the kids, maybe because they'd only just met, or maybe because of his disability. Either way, she had no problem with it. She'd seen him maneuver over the ground just fine, and she could also tell that he was a good disciplinarian of his child. "Thank you. Declan, fifteen minutes. We don't want Lily to get too cold."

"Okay," Declan said impatiently.

"Nice to meet you, and thank you," Vanessa said to the man, shaking his hand. She introduced Evan, and then the boys and Hunter's dad were off toward a pen beside the barn.

She sat back down, Snickers beside her. Evan knelt, helping Lily scoot around in her snowsuit.

"Thank you for being willing to do this," Vanessa said. "I think it's turned out even better than I hoped."

Evan smiled and nodded. "I'm glad the boys worked it out. And Lily had fun. Good stimulation for her."

"It is."

He met her eyes meaningfully. "I had fun, too," he said. "But you realize, we're going to have to spend all evening decorating the monster tree we got."

"It might be a two-day project," she said. She looked into his eyes and got a little lost there.

"I won't mind," he said softly. He didn't look away.

Emotions arced between them.

Snickers let out a yelp, and Vanessa realized Lily had crawled over to the dog and was pulling herself up on his fur.

"Oh, hey, gentle!" Evan scooted over and loosened Lily's fingers, and she started to cry.

Thankful for the distraction of kids and animals, Vanessa took deep breaths to relax.

Being with Evan was more stress on her, but tonight, in this holiday environment, it felt like stress of a good kind.

After wrangling the Christmas tree into the house and setting it up, they took a break for dinner. Afterward, Evan put Lily to bed, loving her smile as he tucked her new doll in beside her.

Getting the Christmas tree and then having dinner made him feel like he and Lily were becoming a family.

Declan went to his room with a *Diary of a Wimpy Kid* book in his hand. His eyes were drooping, though. "I'm guessing he'll be asleep in a few minutes," Evan said to Vanessa when he met her on the landing.

"I think so, too," she said. "Long day for him."

"For you, too. Get some rest. I'm heading up to the attic to get Gramma's Christmas ornaments and whatever other decorations I can find."

"Can I come?" Her eyes sparkled. "Maybe we'll find hidden treasure up there!"

He laughed. "More like a lot of junk," he said. "But if you want to come, you're welcome."

When she followed him up the narrow, winding stairs to the attic, he felt...happy. Just plain happy to spend more time with her. He ought to resist that feeling, or at least analyze it, but…later. He'd do it later.

He pushed open the attic door and was greeted with cool, dusty air. Familiar with the basic layout, he waved a hand through the air and found a string, pulled down on it, and a light bulb came on.

"Wow," Vanessa said behind him. "Lots of stuff."

Boxes were stacked against the side wall, almost as tall as Evan's head. Old furniture clustered in one corner. Blue rubber bins were stacked close to the door. "I'm pretty sure that's what we're looking for," he said, nodding toward them.

Vanessa lifted a lid. "Lots of those old Christmas lights with big bulbs," she said. "Think they're safe?"

"No. I remember burning myself on them. I don't think Gramma's used those in years."

She looked into another box. "Here's a nativity scene," she said, "and a really dusty wreath."

"Let's stack the usable stuff by the door, and I'll carry it down," Evan said. He opened one of the boxes on the side wall. "Oh, wow."

The box was filled with trophies and certificates. He pulled out a small plastic trophy. "'Science Fair Second Place, Chesapeake Corners Middle School,'" he read aloud. "I remember. I was mad I didn't get first place."

"Second is good!" She took the trophy and held it up, smiling. "Keep trying, and maybe one day…"

"Thanks for the encouragement." He chuckled. "Science fair victories don't hold quite the same middle school status as sports ones."

Vanessa knelt beside him. She pulled out a manila envelope brimming with paper. "Can I look?"

"Of course. Gramma had nothing to hide."

"Don't underestimate her," Vanessa teased, but she pulled

out the papers and started looking through them. "Honor Roll, I see," she said, waving a tissue-thin paper at him.

"Back when they did paper report cards. Look at that."

"What's that B for?" She traced a line from the grade to the subject. "Aha. Domestic arts."

"Yeah. I burned everything in cooking class. But I had perfect attendance, and..."

"Ninety nine percent of success is showing up," she said, finishing his sentence. "Or is it 95 percent? I think Woody Allen said it."

He laughed. "It's the only thing that got me through that class."

She pulled out a couple of greeting cards. "Can I look?"

"Sure," he said, and peered over her shoulder.

Mother's Day cards, signed with his messy adolescent signature. He'd written "Gramma" on the envelope. And she'd kept every one, it looked like. He drew in a breath and heaved it out in a sigh. "Let's look through that Christmas stuff," he said.

"Sure." She gave him a quick smile. "Brings it all back, I imagine."

"It does." He walked over and opened a Christmas bin full of ornaments, carefully wrapped in newspaper and paper towels.

Vanessa was looking wistfully through his childhood bins.

"Do you still have stuff from your childhood?" he asked as he started unwrapping the ornaments that looked usable, sturdy enough to be around kids.

"None. After my dad died, we were sort of whisked away from our house. Most of our stuff was lost."

His heart hurt for her. "That was when the foster care started, I guess."

"Right. Only, with two of us, not many would take us together. So we'd get placed separately, and then we'd make plans and run away so we could be together."

The more Evan learned about her upbringing, the more he understood why she had issues. "You and Luke have a close bond."

"He was my rock. But we made the foster families and social workers mad. So...yeah. Lots of transitions. And nobody to put our report cards and crafts into boxes in the attic. No one attic to put them in." She brightened. "But you should see all the stuff I have of Declan's childhood. I have a bin and a photo album for each year of his life. I want him to have a better childhood than I did."

"I think he's having a great childhood, from what I can see," Evan said.

She shook her head rapidly. "I try, but I haven't always been the best. Especially with the eating disorder. That's why I'm so careful about not getting stressed and falling back into it."

They sorted ornaments together for a little while, exclaiming over some beautiful wooden birdhouse ornaments and laughing over a crooked wooden wreath made from popsicle sticks and a couple of discolored candy canes that were, Evan remembered, part of a science activity with borax crystals.

Once they'd finished sorting, Evan started loading the chosen ones into a smaller bin while she poked around the remaining parts of the attic.

"What's this?" she asked. She was holding up an ornate wooden box, about the size of a milk crate.

Just looking at it twisted something in Evan's stomach. He wasn't sure what was in the box, but it somehow made him uncomfortable. He shrugged.

"Mind if I look inside?"

"It's fine." He made himself walk over.

She opened the chest and pulled out a framed photo. "Wow, she's gorgeous! Who is it?"

"My mom." He swallowed hard, seeing those wide eyes. His mother had appeared so sweet and kind, and it was an illusion.

He looked away, then couldn't resist looking back.

Vanessa flipped through more photos, finally landing on one of the same woman with a little boy on a beach, both wearing bathing suits. She held it up, her expression gentle. "You?"

He forced himself to look at the photo. At his own loving, infatuated expression as he looked up at his spectacularly beautiful mother. She wasn't looking at him; she was looking off in the distance, out to sea.

His throat tightened. He remembered that trip. The last one he'd taken with her before she'd left him permanently with Gramma.

There had been a man, and Mom had been head over heels in love with him. They'd sat close together, laughing and kissing when Evan wasn't in the room and acting irritated when he was.

They hadn't wanted to be bothered with a child who got hungry and needed meals and baths and bedtimes. He'd felt his mother's withdrawal and had tried desperately to be good, but to no avail.

It was one of the last times he'd seen her.

He coughed, trying to clear his throat, but it came out as a sort of squawk. "Dusty up here," he croaked out.

Vanessa looked at him with compassionate eyes, then rubbed his arm. "Let's go downstairs and watch a sappy Christmas movie."

"Sure." He was glad to stand, to lift boxes and carry them downstairs. He was glad she hadn't called him on his emotions.

As they settled in with popcorn and cocoa, watching not a sappy movie, but a funny one, he felt better. Because of Vanessa. Somehow, she was helping him to remake his past. And maybe he was helping her with her past a little bit, too.

Wouldn't it be great if they could continue to help each other?

Wouldn't it be great if Vanessa wasn't a deserter, like his mother had been?

Chapter Eight

Saturday morning was the church's Christmas Serenade. Vanessa loved the annual event and was pleased to learn that one of this year's stops was the rehab center where Gramma was staying. Since the center was cautious about visitors and germs, the residents would watch and listen to the families serenading them through the floor-to-ceiling windows in their activity room. That way, everyone could come: grandkids, babies, pets.

Evan was going. So it only made sense that, after spending a little time decorating the Christmas tree, they all drove together. Vanessa's goal was to have a pleasant, conflict-free time with Gramma and her family.

They arrived a little before 10:00 a.m. and gathered with other early arrivals in the parking lot outside the big windows. Evan had brought a big blanket, and he sat Lily down on it with a couple of toys. It was a warm day for December, but Lily was bundled in a hat and coat. Both Vanessa and Evan wore flannel shirts and puffy vests, and Declan laughed at them. "Twinning!" he crowed.

While Evan and Vanessa greeted other families, Declan sat on the blanket with Lily. He put a hand on the baby's feet, encouraging her to push against him, with a "come on, kick me" attitude that was a little rougher than Vanessa would have used. She glanced at Evan, raising an eyebrow. Should they stop Declan or ask him to tone it down? But he just shrugged, smiled and continued to watch.

Declan picked the baby up and sat her on his knee, then lifted her to a standing position, holding her carefully, talking baby talk to her.

Vanessa's heart warmed. Declan would really love to have a younger sibling. But it wasn't going to happen.

"You're good at that," Evan said to Declan.

Declan colored, pleased. "Watch this!" he said. He set Lily down, pulled a colorful stuffed turtle from the diaper bag and set it in front of her, just out of her reach.

Lily leaned toward it, arms extended, and half pushed herself, half fell into an all fours position.

"Come on, get it!" Declan wiggled the toy.

Lily scooted and pulled herself toward the toy. When she reached it, they all cheered. "Wow, that's impressive!" Vanessa said. "You *are* good with her, Declan."

Someone spoke on a loudspeaker. "It's time to get started, everyone. The sound's being piped in to the residents, so sing your hearts out."

Gramma appeared, tugging her chair close to the window, and they all waved. Then they joined in a medley of Christmas carols. In between, a couple of Angie's therapy dogs, wearing red ribbons and in one case, antlers, did tricks.

"Make Snickers do her tricks, Mom!" Declan said.

Vanessa looked down at the dog panting beside her. "Snickers is doing her job right now. Maybe we can show her tricks to Gramma when she comes to visit."

After a few more songs, the program ended and the residents applauded. Evan took Lily right up to the window, and Gramma pressed her hand to it. It was heartwarming and sweet.

"Time for me to do some heavy lifting," Evan said, "if you can keep an eye on Lily for a few." They'd brought cartons of gifts for the residents of the rehab center, and Evan had volunteered to unload the truck.

"I can help," Declan offered.

"Great. We could use your muscles."

The two of them walked off together, and Vanessa's heart squeezed.

She was happy their rift had healed. She sat on the blanket with Lily and patted her lap for Snickers to join them. She needed the comfort of her service dog to keep from giving too much of her heart to a man who would never approve of her if he knew the truth about her.

After the morning event, and an afternoon visit with Gramma—he and Lily were sneaked in by a sympathetic nurse—Evan should have been happy.

Instead he got home and retreated with Lily to their suite, feeling lonely.

All day, he'd been seeing families with Mom, Dad and kids.

He hadn't come from a so-called intact family, but he'd always longed for one, deep inside.

That longing lay behind his past relationship with Vanessa, in which he'd let himself get so emotionally attached so quickly. And it lay behind his overhasty marriage to his wife.

After those two disasters, he'd concluded that marriage and family life weren't for him.

Okay. Fine, he'd decided. He would stay single. Contribute to society through his work. Indeed, his work had consumed most of his energy. He'd gotten a little obsessive about it.

But everything had changed when he'd learned he was

a father. When he'd held Lily for the first time. When he'd started caring for her.

He wanted more for his daughter. More than he, an ignorant forty-year-old man, could provide for a baby girl who'd grow up to be a woman. He wanted her to have a mother who'd teach her how to navigate the choppy waters of female adolescence. Who'd show her how to be strong and nurturing at the same time.

If there had been any notion in his head that his ex-wife could provide that for Lily, it had been destroyed when he'd learned that Lily had been neglected on her watch. No way was Frederika getting anywhere near Lily. He didn't even care any longer whether Lily was his biological child. He was going to care for her, and Frederika was out of the picture.

Which left him at an impasse.

He wanted a real family for Lily, a family complete with a mother. Maybe even a sibling. Witness how much she loved Declan.

How much she was coming to love Vanessa, too.

One thing was for sure: he'd tried and failed in forming a relationship with Vanessa years ago, and he'd be a fool to repeat the same mistake.

After putting Lily to bed, he wandered out to the living room in his old flannels and a worn-out Temple University T-shirt. His plan was to find a football game or some mindless show on TV.

He smelled bread baking and heard off-key singing. It was as if Gramma had come home and taken up the role she'd played throughout his childhood.

He padded into the kitchen in his thick socks. Of course it wasn't Gramma; it was Vanessa.

She wore practically the same outfit he was wearing, old flannels and a fitted T-shirt. She was kneeling in front of her dog. "Sit pretty," she said to him, and he rose up and balanced, precariously, on his back end. "Good boy!" she said and tossed him a treat.

"Smells good in here," Evan said, and Vanessa jumped. "Oh, man, you scared me," she said.

"What are you doing?" he asked.

"Multitasking," she said promptly. "I'm trying to teach Snickers to do some of the tricks that Angie's dog does. And I'm meal prepping, so I have something healthy to eat for lunches next week." She held out a hand, displaying five glass storage containers full of what looked and smelled like vegetable soup. "Oh, and I'm baking bread. And wrapping Declan's gifts." She nodded toward the wrapping paper, scissors and tape on the kitchen table.

"Impressive." He sank into a chair at the table.

She studied him for a moment. Then she sliced a couple of pieces of fresh bread from the loaf cooling on the counter. She pulled butter out of the fridge and put it on the table in front of him, along with a knife. "Fresh, hot bread with butter always makes Declan feel better. Maybe it'll work for you."

"Thanks." He buttered the bread and took a bite. Nodded. "This could work," he said, and took another bite.

In fact, he already did feel better, being in the room with Vanessa. Which was dangerous, but he didn't have the energy to fight that desire for connection in himself.

She took half a slice of bread for herself, spread it with a touch of butter and sat down opposite him. "What's wrong?" she asked.

He shrugged. "Just...getting some holiday blues, I guess. Seeing all those happy families today... You know."

"I do know," she said promptly. "Why do you think I'm baking and wrapping and teaching the dog tricks?"

"Where's Declan?" he asked. The kid was a pain at times, but he generally added levity to a room.

"Sleepover at his friend Josiah's house," she said. "He likes being over there where there's mom and dad and kids. And grandparents and uncles and cousins. It's something I can't provide for him."

"Yeah." He sighed. "I'm just starting to realize the challenges of being a single parent. They don't stop when they get to school age, huh?"

She laughed. "Not hardly."

They sat companionably for a few minutes. Snickers came over and flopped heavily down between them, resting his muzzle on his paws.

"So can I ask you something?" He regretted the words as soon as they were out of his mouth.

"Sure. Although I can't promise I'll answer."

Having gotten this far, he went for it. "When you told me you never wanted to see me again, twelve years ago…why was that? Had you met someone else?"

"No." She studied his face for a moment and then shook her head. "No. I hadn't met someone else."

"Then why…"

"It's hard to explain." She thought for a moment, then spoke again. "I guess I felt like we were from different worlds."

That sounded like an excuse. "Not really. You came from foster care. I happened to have a grandmother who took care of me. We were both out a couple of biological parents."

"But you were raised to be a good person," she said. "Gramma taught you well. Whereas I…"

He waited.

"I was more…lost. Maybe it was a weakness in me, but I couldn't seem to figure out how families were supposed to work or how to have a good relationship. I didn't even see the value of trying until I had Declan."

"Okay," he said, thinking he should drop it. But the truth was, he wanted to say more, to talk it through, at least a little bit. Maybe it was the lateness of the hour or the fact that, aside from Lily, they were alone in the house. "I was broken up about it when you dumped me," he admitted. "I thought our relationship could go somewhere. Thought we might be headed for a happily-ever-after."

"I know you did," she said slowly. "That's why I had to leave."

"What?" That made absolutely no sense.

"You were too good," she said. "Too wholesome. I knew I couldn't live up to what you wanted me to be, so I got out before I got any more attached."

He frowned. He didn't want to question her words, but he was having trouble believing them.

She gave him a faint smile. "If it helps, I was pretty broken up about it, too."

"Really?" He sliced more bread and handed a piece to her, then took two for himself.

It was dark outside, warm and cozy in the kitchen. The only sound was Snickers's heavy breathing. The bread tasted like home.

Evan didn't feel comfortable with many women. He was more of a man's man, always had been. But here, tonight, even talking about a difficult topic, he felt comfortable with Vanessa.

"I should have a glass of milk," she said suddenly. She got up and poured herself a glass, then held up the carton. "Want some?"

"Sure," he said, and she poured another glass and brought both over to the table.

"I have low bone density because of the eating disorder," she explained. "I try to get as much calcium as I can."

"I didn't know that was a symptom," he said. Obviously she wanted to change the subject, and she was entitled to do that.

"More of a consequence. The good side effect of it all is Snickers." She reached down and scratched the dog's ears.

A sound came from Lily's room, then a little cry. They both stood at the same moment. "I'll get her," he said, but Vanessa tagged along.

When they got to Lily's bedroom, the baby was sitting up in her crib. He walked over to her.

"Da-da," she said, clear as anything.

He gasped and turned back to Vanessa. "Did you hear that?"

"She called you Da-da! Is that the first time she's said it?"

"It is." Evan reached into the crib and patted her. His heart felt like it was swelling right out of his chest, and his throat tightened. "Smart girl," he managed to choke out.

"Brilliant girl," Vanessa said, beside him. "I'm so excited she said your name!"

Lily seemed to read their appreciation. "Da-Da, Da-Da," she singsonged.

His heart was full. He'd never known any sweetness like hearing his daughter call him Da-da. He picked her up and lifted her high into the air.

"I hate to say it," Vanessa said, "but we probably shouldn't get her all riled up. She'll never fall asleep."

"True." He brought her back down and tucked her into the crook of his arm.

"Tell you what, I'll rock her and you read to her. She likes to hear your voice."

"She does?"

"She does."

So Vanessa sat in the rocker, holding Lily and gently rocking her. Evan read to her from a way-too-advanced picture book about a doll that hadn't been chosen for Christmas.

Sure enough, within five minutes Lily was asleep, and Vanessa placed her gently in her crib.

They walked down the hall, shutting the door halfway.

"I should go clean up the kitchen," she said.

Evan should go to bed. But instead, he touched her arm. "Thank you," he said.

"For what?" She was standing close to him.

He could see the tiny mole on her cheek, could smell the citrusy scent of the shampoo she used, mixed with the smell of baking bread.

"For helping Lily. For helping me feel better. For making this a home."

Her eyes teared up. A tear spilled over.

He caught it with his thumb, then stroked her cheek. "What's this about?"

"It's what I want more than anything. To make a home. For Declan. And… I'm glad it feels that way for you, too."

"I want that for Lily."

"It's not easy," she said.

"No." They were still close together. He was still touching her face, and then he couldn't help it: he pulled her into a hug. "Is this okay?" he asked and felt her nod.

This was good. It was a hug, like they'd done before. No more.

Only he wanted more. He lifted his head and looked into her eyes. "Can I kiss you?" he heard himself say.

"Oh, Evan." She bit her lip. Then she nodded.

And he did.

Chapter Nine

As Evan's mouth brushed hers, light and gentle, Vanessa felt her shoulders relax.

This was Evan. Respectful, gentle, nonthreatening. Kind. Good. She closed her eyes.

His fingertip brushed her neck. "You're beautiful," he breathed against her mouth. He kissed her again, more firmly.

Her heart pounded faster. She should put a stop to this, for reasons she couldn't quite remember. But she didn't. Instead, she wrapped her arms around his neck and tangled her fingers in his hair.

He pulled her closer. "If you tell me to stop, I'll stop," he said as he tucked her against his broad chest. "I don't want to push you into anything, it's just... I can't resist you right now."

She leaned against him, turning her face to the side, hearing his heartbeat. She could tell him to stop. She should. She would, in just one minute.

She just needed a little bit more of this comfort, this strength, this caring that she felt with his arms wrapped around her.

He stroked her hair, gently, like she was a precious treasure.

She looked up and kissed the corner of his mouth. And

then he was kissing her, deep and dizzying, and she had no choice but to cling on. She'd fall otherwise.

At the same moment, they pulled apart. He looked down at her, his eyes dark as obsidian, his breathing labored. She stared back at him.

Wow. This was nothing like the gentle kisses they'd shared before.

This was dangerous. She took a step back. "Uh...it might be a good idea to..."

"Right. We can't do this." He reached out and traced a finger over her lips. "But just so you know, I really want to."

She nodded. "Me, too."

They stared at each other for a few more seconds, and then she pulled herself away and turned and walked out to the kitchen, her heart pounding, a smile that wouldn't quit on her face.

Maybe things could change.

Maybe *she* had changed enough to have a relationship with a good man.

Vanessa's good mood lasted through the night, through picking Declan up from his sleepover, through the church service. Outside, the weather had turned gray and cold, but inside, the sun shone bright. Oh, she was nervous, a little, warning herself not to get too excited, to take it slow, play it at least a little cool. She was glad to have Snickers beside her, his large body half sprawled under the pew. She reached down and touched his soft ears, gave him a scratch.

She couldn't forget how Evan had looked at her, how he'd touched her with tender authority. The idea of entrusting herself, her whole self, to a man like Evan was intoxicating.

As the closing music played and people started standing, she pulled herself out of her happy daze so she could pay attention to what her son was saying. "They needed coaches, and they said to ask your dad or your uncle or whoever," Declan said, "so I asked him."

"You asked who?"

"Evan! Mom, pay attention!" He grinned; he was joking.

A tendril of worry wound around Vanessa's stomach and tightened.

If she and Evan got closer, Evan and Declan would get closer, too. It was already happening. Which was a good thing, a very good thing, what she wanted.

Except…what if things didn't work out? At some point, she'd have to tell Evan the story of Declan's conception. Would that cause him to back away and hurt Declan?

But he'd been so loving last night. Surely he'd understand.

Evan was chatting to someone in the back of the church. He didn't have Lily with him, which meant she was probably still in the nursery. "I'm going to pick up Lily," she said to Declan.

"I'm gonna ask Caleb if he wants to play basketball, too," Declan said.

"Don't go far," she called after her son.

With Snickers walking beside her, she got Lily from the nursery—Evan had added her as a caregiver with permission to pick up for him—and then headed back toward the sanctuary, slowly. She carried Lily on her hip, the weight of her a pleasant pressure. *Aw, little one, I could mother you.*

Talk about getting ahead of herself! She straightened her back and walked briskly over to where Evan was standing, talking to Gramma's next-door neighbor.

Evan gave Vanessa a special smile as he greeted her and took Lily from her arms. Most of the people had trickled out by now, but Angie and Luke were at the other side of the sanctuary with their three foster kids.

"Now, there's a redemption story," Mrs. Fenstermaker said, nodding toward Angie and Luke.

"How so?" Evan asked.

"She was married to Oscar Anderson," Mrs. Fenstermaker said.

Evan nodded. "I've met him. I'm surprised he and Angie were married."

"It was a mismatch," Mrs. Fenstermaker said. "Don't you think, Vanessa? She was so much younger than he was. And there were a lot of negative rumors about him." She smacked the side of her head, lightly. "Listen to me, gossiping in church. I'm just glad her life is so much better now. It's a God thing."

Sweat dripped down Vanessa's back. She looked away from the pair of them, trying to collect herself. She checked Declan's location—he was laughing at something his friend Caleb had said.

At her side, Snickers leaned against her.

She touched the dog's shaggy head for comfort. Her heart pounded so hard that Snickers, at least, could probably hear it. Or feel the stress rolling off her body in waves. Smell the sweat.

Don't overreact. Maybe he won't be judgmental.

After Mrs. Fenstermaker left, Evan looked at Vanessa, smiling a little. "I'm so tempted to put my arm around you right now," he said.

Heat rose to her face. What she wouldn't give for a man who'd put his arm around her in church.

He glanced in the direction Mrs. Fenstermaker had gone. "I can't believe Angie was married to that sleazy guy, Oscar," he said. "My colleagues said he ran around with all kinds of, well, not-so-great women while he was married. That must have been awful for her."

He was waiting for a response.

"Yeah," she choked out.

"I mean, I just don't get why a man would go with *that* kind of woman when he had someone like Angie."

That kind of woman.

He wasn't wrong. Angie had been a wonderful wife to Oscar, from everything Vanessa had learned after the fact. When Angie had learned about her husband's unfaithfulness, after his death, she'd been devastated.

Vanessa had been *that kind of woman*. The other woman. Moreover, she'd gotten pregnant. Angie, the legitimate wife, had wanted desperately to have children with Oscar, and he'd refused.

From the outside—from Evan's point of view—Vanessa had been part of a whole sinful, destructive pattern. And it wasn't just from Evan's point of view; she *had* sinned. She'd accepted the attention of a wealthy older man, not because she had loved him, but because she'd been lonely and weak. She'd entered into a relationship with him without a thought for building things slowly, for being friends first, for getting to know one another well. Waiting for marriage before becoming intimate hadn't even been on her radar at that time in her life.

If she'd done things right, she'd have probed into Oscar's background. She'd have noticed that he was secretive and unavailable. She'd have figured out that he was married and brushed him off instantly.

And then she wouldn't have had Declan, wonderful Declan. God had worked it all for good.

But there was a cost. She could never have a relationship with a good, moral man like Evan.

All of Vanessa's foolish hopes whooshed out of her. Of course this wasn't going to work. She didn't dare let Evan get close to Declan. She felt sick, imagining the things he could say to her son. About Oscar, his father. About Vanessa herself.

Best to back off now. She straightened her spine and forced herself to look at him with coolness. "Hey, I know Declan asked you to coach his game today," she said, hearing the flatness of her own voice. "I'd rather you didn't. It's better for all of us if we keep things professional."

"But I thought—"

She shook her head rapidly. "We weren't thinking clearly last night. It's just way too complicated. Like I said, let's keep things professional."

Hurt flashed across his face.

She hated causing that. But better a little hurt now than a lot of it later. Better to hurt an adult who could handle it than to open the door to bigger hurt for her young, vulnerable son.

After church and that weird, disturbing conversation with Vanessa, Evan drove home with Lily and got them both lunch.

Why had Vanessa said she didn't want him with Declan and that they should keep things professional? Right before that, she'd seemed warm and enthusiastic. And last night, she'd seemed very into their kiss.

He had been, too. It had been…amazing. Amazing and yet sweet. It had left him hopeful and sleepless and cautiously optimistic about what might come about between them.

But she'd cut it off and backed away. Now, he felt like a chump.

He'd thought for a minute there that they had something, or were going to build something.

He'd been wrong. His mistake had been trusting a woman for even the length of a kiss.

He was an idiot, he thought as he cut leftover chicken into baby-sized bites for Lily. Vanessa had somehow trapped him for a second time, then shoved him away and stomped on his heart. Had she done it for fun?

"We'd dump her if we could," he said to Lily.

"Da-da," she said, then broke into her usual string of babbling.

He couldn't dump Vanessa, though. He had several meetings and some important reports to work on this week. He needed her to take care of Lily. And bad as she was for him, he knew she was good for Lily. She understood Lily's needs and was working with her well, and they were making progress.

He wiped Lily off and put her down for a nap. The time flew by as he got some remote work done. Then she was up again, and he played with her and talked to her and got her a snack.

He put her down to play some more, and she crawled rapidly across the floor. That was new, and very good. Except...

"No, not the dog food!" He rushed to her in time to prevent her from putting a piece of Snickers's kibble into her mouth.

There was a bustle at the back door, and Vanessa and Declan came in, with Snickers following along. The dog shook himself and then walked over to his bowl and started eating, as if he knew Lily had been about to steal his dinner.

Declan was his usual cheerful self, greeting Evan and picking up Lily.

Evan felt a twist in his gut. He really liked that kid. Declan liked him, too, and looked up to him, or was starting to.

Their relationship was just another casualty of a woman's fickleness.

Vanessa walked across the kitchen, not looking at Evan.

"Come on, Declan, get your shower while I fix us some dinner."

"I'll shower later."

"Declan..."

"Fine." The boy started to huff off.

The doorbell rang.

"I'll get it," Vanessa said, and headed to the door. Evan walked to the entryway to see who was visiting as twilight approached on a Sunday evening.

"We're here!" Luke, Angie and their three kids poured into the house.

Vanessa looked at Evan, her forehead wrinkling. "I forgot," she mouthed to him.

He'd forgotten, too, that they'd said something about hosting the other family for dinner tonight.

Of course they'd forgotten. They'd been occupied with other things, like kissing.

Somehow, they had to get through the evening. "I was just about to order the pizza," he said.

Relief crossed Vanessa's face. "That would be great. And I'm going to make a salad in just a few."

"We brought brownies and ice cream," Angie said.

"Yeah," their foster son said, "and she wouldn't let us eat any of it."

"After dinner," Angie said, ruffling the boy's hair.

"Come on, I'll show you my new game," Declan said, and the two boys followed him to his room.

That left Evan to hang coats. "Come sit by the fire," Vanessa said to their remaining guests. "The little ones can play together." Angie and Luke's third foster child was a little girl named Charlotte, just slightly bigger than Lily. She plopped down on the floor beside Lily's stacking rings and grabbed the top one.

Lily started to reach for the same ring, but Evan quickly distracted her with her favorite doll.

Vanessa came over to him while Angie and Luke were occupied with the little ones. "Thanks for the pizza idea," she said.

"Sure." He couldn't look at her. She was too pretty and he was too angry with her.

"Just order a lot of pizza. Those boys look hungry."

"Sure you don't mind me being around Declan?" he asked sarcastically.

"We'll talk," she said. She didn't rise to the bait, but he noticed she was stroking a lock of her hair, over and over. She was nervous. Well, good.

Angie picked up the brownies and ice cream, and the women headed for the kitchen. Evan sat on the couch, watching Lily and Charlotte as they played side by side.

Luke sat at the other end of the couch. "Everything okay, man?"

Evan looked over at him, surprised. They weren't really even friends. They'd only met a couple of times.

Apparently, though, it was enough for Luke to see that something was wrong with Evan.

"Just a stressful time," he said. "And situation." He waved a hand in a circle to indicate the house, the babies and the kitchen.

"Yeah?"

"Family-like, but not," Evan clarified. He grabbed the remote and turned on the TV. Sunday night football ought to cover any awkwardness.

"Any chance of it becoming *more* family-like?" Luke asked.

"Nope."

"You and Vanessa getting along okay?"

Evan knew Luke was probing because he was protective of his sister. "She's good with Lily," he said mildly.

Luke gave him a hard glare. "You know, if having Vanessa live here in the same house is causing any problems, she'll always have a place with me. Declan, too. Just say the word. Or she can. I'll speak with her, too."

It was the most he'd ever heard Luke say. "I need her for Lily," Evan said. "Aside from that, I'm treating her with respect, like the professional she is."

"See that you do," Luke said.

They both turned their attention to the TV. But a cooling-off period of sports watching was not in their future. Declan and the other two boys ran through the room at full speed, nearly trampling the babies. A lamp would have been knocked over if Luke hadn't caught it.

"Sorry." Declan knelt beside Lily. "You okay, baby?" he asked, tickling her leg until she laughed.

"Apologize to Mr. Dukas," Luke told his foster sons, and they did.

"It might be a good idea to throw a football around outside," Evan suggested.

"Yeah!" Declan said.

"Cool!"

The boys started out the door. "Wait," Luke said. "Jackets and boots." He assisted with getting the boys bundled up.

That left Evan to take the little girls into the kitchen. He propped Lily on his hip and took the other little girl's hand. "We're taking the boys outside for the sake of the furniture," he said to the two women. Then he looked at Vanessa. "If that's okay? We're going to play ball." He held her eye, baiting her.

"Of course. Thank you."

"You're sure?" he asked, keeping his voice low. "Earlier today, you didn't seem to want me to play ball with him."

"Yes, Evan. Go."

Her expression was tight. Snickers roused himself and trotted over to stand beside her, and she reached down and rested a hand on the dog's head.

Evan headed outside. He didn't feel particularly satisfied by getting in a dig at Vanessa. In fact, he felt like a jerk.

It was going to be a long evening. A very long holiday season.

Chapter Ten

Vanessa guided Lily and little Charlotte to a corner of the kitchen, safely away from knives and appliances, while Angie continued chopping carrots and radishes. Outside, Evan and Luke and the boys played football, regardless of the fact that it was twenty-eight degrees and getting dark.

Angie looked out the window and laughed. "They're falling all over the place in that half inch of snow. They'll be a mess when they come in, for sure."

"I'd better put a heap of towels by the door." Vanessa didn't mind mopping up after them. She was glad Declan had kids to play with, and men like her brother—and Evan, she supposed—to mentor and supervise. And she was glad they were outside, away from her—especially Evan.

Her heart ached every time she looked at him. That kiss had been so sweet, so wonderful, so promising. And then she'd come back down to earth. When she'd heard him talk disparagingly of Oscar and his side chicks, she'd realized that he would never accept her background.

She dumped a couple of dolls and a container of blocks into the makeshift play area she'd created by turning a couple of chairs on their sides. Then she helped the two little girls get settled there. Snickers lay outside of the enclosure, nose on paws, eyes flickering from the little girls to the food prep taking place at the counter.

Vanessa just wanted to get through this evening without too much stress. One day at a time. She showed Lily how to stack one block on top of the other, something Angie's little girl had already mastered. "I hope playing with your Charlotte will help Lily gain some new skills," she said.

Angie stopped chopping and turned. "You're starting to love her, aren't you?"

"I am," Vanessa admitted. "I can't resist. I can resist her dad, but not her."

"Why do you want to resist her dad?" Angie asked. "You two seem to have a lot in common."

After a last glance at the toddlers, Vanessa walked over and started setting the kitchen table. "It's an awkward topic."

"Uh-oh. You don't have to share the personal details."

Vanessa laughed nervously. "Not that kind of awkward. It's more about...our past. Yours and mine."

Curiosity darkened Angie's eyes. "It's okay. Go for it."

Vanessa drew in a breath. She needed to talk to someone, and only Angie knew the whole story. "Well... I was starting to trust Evan. I felt like I could be vulnerable with him. Felt worthy of him."

"Of course you're worthy of him!" Angie frowned. "Why would you think otherwise?"

"Oh, you know. The old self-esteem stuff, and I'm working to overcome that. But something he said..." She trailed off, then spoke again. "It was about Oscar."

Angie's eyebrows shot up practically to her hairline. "What did he say?"

Now that she'd started, Vanessa had to spit it all out. "He knew Oscar, remember? From some fundraiser. Someone in church brought up that you used to be married to him, and

Evan's reaction… Well. He said he felt sorry for you, because of Oscar's reputation for running around with sleazy women."

"Oh, honey." Angie bit her lip, her eyes sad. "That must have been hard to hear. It's hard for me to hear."

"Yeah." They'd both loved Oscar once. Angie had had the worst of the deal, being married to a man who turned out to have cheated on her with multiple women. Vanessa had been one of them.

"You're not sleazy, though. You know that, right? You didn't realize he was married."

"And you're the only woman I know who could possibly be kind and friendly to a woman who was with her husband. And had a child by him." Vanessa looked at beautiful Angie, now a dear friend as well as her sister-in-law, and marveled at her grace and ability to forgive.

"You know what? It doesn't even hurt anymore. God has blessed me so much." She looked out the window, and then over at the little girls playing quietly. Her eyes crinkled with a soft smile.

"He's blessed my brother even more. You're so good for him."

"I'm thankful every day." She came over and gave Vanessa a quick hug. "I want this kind of happiness for you, too. Is it worth a try, telling Evan the whole story?"

Vanessa hugged Angie back, then stepped away. "No. I don't see how. I've committed to be Lily's nanny throughout the holidays. Declan and I need the housing and the money, and Evan needs me to care for Lily. I don't want to rock the boat by telling him stuff that may make him kick us out." She sighed. "I think it's better for us to keep a distance and skim along the surface. I can't get more involved with Evan."

"But you'd like to?"

Vanessa thought a minute. "In a perfect world... I'd like to see where things could go. In the real world, there are too many chances for Declan's and my lives to go straight downhill." She felt despair as she said it.

Snickers stood, shook himself and came over to stand by Vanessa.

"Snickers is amazing," Angie said. "He really senses when you need comfort, doesn't he?"

"He does." Vanessa knelt and hugged him, which he accepted patiently. "He's the only guy for me, aren't you?"

The doorbell rang, and then the front door opened. "Pizza's here," someone called. And then there was a flurry of drying off and wiping feet, stacking boots by the door, getting the little girls' hands cleaned off and settling everyone at the table. They prayed, and then everyone dug in.

A large pizza was on plates and consumed within two minutes, and they got well into a second and then a third before everyone started slowing down. The smell of pepperoni and mushrooms and tomato sauce filled the room. Vanessa walked around putting salad into everyone's bowl, though she could see it wouldn't disappear nearly as quickly as pizza did.

"Did you try out for wrestling?" one of Luke and Angie's boys asked Declan around a mouthful of pizza.

"Nah." Declan grabbed another piece. "I didn't want to. I probably wouldn't have made it."

"Why do you think that?" Luke asked him.

Declan shrugged. "I'm just not that strong," he said.

Vanessa's heart hurt just hearing her son say that. "You're strong," she said. "You're good at sports, a lot of them, anyway."

He shrugged and looked away, and Vanessa frowned. When had Declan lost his confidence in himself as an athlete?

"If you feel like you need to gain strength, there are things you can do about it," Evan said. "You can lift weights, run, do push-ups."

Declan looked hopeful for a moment and then shook his head. "It's too hard."

The conversation moved on. Everyone was talking at once and grabbing for more pizza, and it was fun and lively, what Vanessa wanted her home and her table to be like. But she couldn't enjoy it.

Had she caused Declan to lose confidence? Did she model an attitude of not being strong?

It wasn't even a question. That was exactly what she'd done.

Her heart thudded painfully as she looked down at her pizza, grease congealing on the top of it.

Snickers nudged her. She wasn't sure if the dog was begging or telling her to eat.

She realized she hadn't eaten lunch. Did she have breakfast? Yes, she'd had fruit and yogurt before church.

She took a tiny bite of pizza and then rubbed Snickers's head.

Having an empty stomach felt good. Strong. In control.

Everyone was eating and talking, having a good time. Evan laughed at something one of the boys said, throwing his head back. He was so handsome. So appealing.

So not for her.

Luke was sitting on Declan's other side, and he reached around his nephew to touch Vanessa's arm. "Aren't you going to eat?" he asked quietly.

"I'm fine!" she snapped. Then she gave her brother a reassuring smile. One of Luke's foster sons caught Luke's attention, thankfully.

She put her piece of pizza on Declan's plate.

Just for today, to get through it, she decided, she didn't have to eat. She knew just how to get away with it. She spread a little salad on her plate, took a forkful and held it while she chatted with Angie. Soon, Lily got fussy, and she took the baby in her lap, feeding her bits of pizza and rocking her, comforting her. When Snickers nudged at her, she sneaked a few bites of pizza to him. Snickers was trained, but he wasn't perfect. He wouldn't resist yummy, meaty food that was handed to him.

Let Evan judge her for her past, shame her for her mistakes. Let Luke scold her to the point where she had to sneak around. She could handle it.

She might not be able to make her life turn out the way she wanted, but she could keep herself thin and empty. Sometimes, that was the best she could do.

On Monday morning, with the help of an aide and a nurse, Evan got Gramma into his car for a visit home. After a flurry of warnings and cautionary statements, they were off.

"Whew, those health care ladies are some strong women," Gramma said. "I feel inspired every time I see them or work with them."

"How are you feeling, really?"

"Restless," she said. "I know I need the physical therapy, and I've been working hard at it, but I want to come home."

"Understandable." He steered out of the parking lot and onto the highway.

The sky was blue, the trees sparkling with a thin coating of ice.

"It's so beautiful out here in God's creation," Gramma said. "Thank you for springing me for a few hours. I really appreciate it."

"It's the least I can do." Truthfully, Evan was glad to get out of the house.

He'd wondered whether he and Vanessa would get close again after they'd worked together last night to host their surprise guests. But as soon as everyone had left, she'd cleaned up and gone to bed without a word to him. This morning, she'd been cool and professional. She might have been a nanny from one of those agencies he'd tried unsuccessfully to reach, for as personal as she acted with him.

He couldn't blame her, not really. He'd been cold to her last night, when he wasn't baiting her.

Gramma studied him, and because he'd grown up with her, he could feel her shrewd eyes on him. "What?" he asked.

"How's it going with Vanessa?" she asked.

He couldn't put his emotions about Vanessa into words, wasn't sure he wanted to. "She's good with Lily."

"Any problems related to your past together? Do the two of you ever talk about it?"

They were reaching the edge of Chesapeake Corners now, and he stopped at a light and watched as a couple of bundled-up women crossed the street. "It's awkward," he said.

Gramma chuckled. "You always *were* a little awkward with women."

"Thanks a lot."

"No, it's understandable. Your mom was unreliable. Your dad wasn't much better. And then you had that science and tech bent. That field is dominated by men."

"Right." He turned the corner, and they drove slowly through the downtown. Even though it was a weekday, the street was fairly crowded with cars and pedestrians. Christmas shopping, he supposed. Which he needed to do, and soon.

"That's why I liked you and Vanessa together," Gramma said. "You weren't awkward with her."

Evan didn't answer, but her words made him think.

It was true, actually. Vanessa didn't have the giggling, girlie attitude that always made Evan feel like women were speaking a language he didn't understand.

"You know," Gramma said, "you're going to have to overcome your attitude toward women if you want to find love, eventually."

"It won't be with Vanessa." He waved a mother pushing a stroller across the street.

"Can't you forgive her?"

"No! And I can't believe you can."

"Oh, honey." She patted his arm. "When you get to be as old as I am, you realize that holding on to old grudges is a waste of time. I was plenty mad when Vanessa broke things off with you, but as I've gotten to know her, I've started to understand why she did it."

"Why'd she do it?" The question burst out of him, destroying any impression of him not caring about her. But he was too curious for his grandmother's wise perspective to pretend indifference.

Gramma shook her head. "She had a lot in her background that made her feel less than others. She doesn't think she deserves love, even now." She paused, then added, "I wonder if you have some of the same issues."

"Humph." Evan didn't answer. He was starting to wonder if getting Gramma out was a good idea. He loved her, but her questions could be probing, leading to uncomfortable feelings about himself.

She seemed to recognize that he'd gone as far as he could with the Vanessa talk. She didn't let up on the personal stuff, though. "You mentioned DNA testing for Lily," she said as they turned onto their street. "Have you started that in motion?"

"No. Haven't had time." He pulled the car into the driveway and turned to face her. "To be honest, I want Lily either way. No matter my deficiencies, with babies and women and otherwise, I'll still be better than my ex at raising her."

Gramma's face broke into a broad smile. "That's my boy," she said. "And I know you can overcome any weaknesses you have, if you work on it. Now, help me out of the car. I want to see my great-grandbaby."

As he assisted Gramma, a woman came out of the house, carrying a case of materials. "I'm Deidre, early intervention," she said as she hastened to her hatchback. "Schedule change. I stopped by early on the chance I could work with Lily now instead of later, and your caregiver said it was okay. You must be Dad and Great-Gramma. Can't stop to talk, but I hope to see you next time."

They barely had a chance to greet her and she was gone.

They went inside, and Evan got the familiar lurch in his stomach when he saw Vanessa. She looked good to him, even though objectively, she looked bad. Dark circles under her eyes and old sweats hanging on her thin torso. "Hey," she said. "I barely got the baby ready in time for the early intervention lady. Hi, Gramma, I'll hug you later. I need to comb my hair and put on something presentable." She didn't speak to Evan, she just made her way slowly up the stairs, leaning on the railing. Snickers trotted after her.

Evan watched her for a moment, frowning, then settled Gramma in a comfortable chair and brought Lily over.

Gramma smiled. "She is your daughter for certain," she said. "She's just like you were as a baby, around the eyes."

There was sudden loud barking upstairs. Snickers ran halfway down the stairs, then back up.

"You'd better see—" Gramma started.

"I'm going to check on her." Evan ran upstairs.

There was Vanessa, on the floor. Struggling to sit up.

"What happened? Did you pass out?" He knelt and helped her while Snickers bustled around them, panting. He leaned Vanessa against the wall. "What can I get you?"

Vanessa didn't answer, seeming dazed. Gramma was at the bottom of the stairs. "If she's not been eating, she needs to get her blood sugar up," she called. "I'll pour her some orange juice."

He made sure Vanessa was stable, ran down and took the glass from Gramma. Orange juice and a straw. He rushed back up and held it to Vanessa's mouth.

She sipped, then sipped again. "Thanks," she said.

She was looking at him, not distantly, but not real alertly, either. Against his will, he felt for her. Was this a manifestation of her eating disorder? He tried to remember whether she'd eaten much lately. He just wasn't sure.

"Do you want to get in bed, or go downstairs and rest on the couch?" he asked her. "Gramma and I will take care of Lily." He was glad Declan was at school. Seeing his mom like this would be scary, although he supposed Declan had seen her that way before.

"Thanks. I'll come down. I want to see Gramma." She tried to get to her feet, but swayed and sank partway back down.

Evan hurried to help her. Slowly, they made their way down the stairs, with Evan on one side and Snickers on the other.

Gramma gave her a gentle hug. "You'll need to be calling your therapist," she warned.

"I will," Vanessa said faintly. "Thank you. Both of you."

Was she still cold toward him? He couldn't tell.

Somehow, that didn't seem as important when her health was at risk. What would have happened if he and Gramma hadn't been here?

With everything in him, he wanted to help her. The trouble was, he wasn't sure she'd want or accept his help.

Chapter Eleven

A couple hours after her fainting episode, they went to the Books-n-Brews Café in downtown Chesapeake Corners.

Vanessa felt like she had an extra service dog. His name was Evan, and he was way more concerned about her than Snickers was.

They were taking Gramma back to her rehab, but at her request, they'd stopped to do a little Christmas shopping and have lunch.

If lunch was what you could call it. More like a gargantuan feast.

Evan had insisted that she and Gramma, along with Lily, sit down while he ordered. That made sense. Gramma had a close contact cast with a boot for her broken ankle. She was allowed to walk but was limited in terms of time and distance. Vanessa could tell that the older woman was tired after the visit home and the drama Vanessa had caused with her fainting episode.

Lily was in a social mood, waving at the other diners and looking around, wide-eyed, at the sparkly Christmas decorations.

Evan brought over a huge tray of sandwiches and pastries, then went back to collect three fancy coffee drinks for them, plus a little carton of juice for Lily. Beneath Vanessa's chair,

Snickers kept bumping and nudging her. Hard to know if the pup wanted to check on Vanessa or check out the delicious-smelling food.

As Evan sat down, he cast a concerned look toward Vanessa. Gramma glanced at her, too, as if to check on her reaction to all the food.

Vanessa could hardly blame them all for worrying. She was worried herself.

Fasting had seemed like a good idea at first. She'd felt empowered last night, and again this morning when she'd overcome her hunger pangs and eaten next to nothing. A few bites of salad last night, a single strawberry this morning.

One part of her, her thinking brain, had known all along that she was being foolish and unhealthy. Avoiding food was not empowering. Even if she'd needed to lose weight for her health, starving wasn't the right way to do it. And she *didn't* need to lose weight. Her doctor had recommended that she gain ten pounds.

But the tension and intensity and uncertainty surrounding her relationship with Evan had temporarily taken away her common sense. Nothing empowering about that.

Just look at what had happened: she'd gotten lightheaded and nearly fainted. Descending back into her eating disorder made her weak, not strong.

"This is a ridiculous amount of food," Gramma said. "We won't eat half of it."

Evan sat down and started passing out sandwiches. "I, for one, am starving. What we don't eat, we'll take home." He didn't start eating, though. Instead he watched, worriedly, as Vanessa unwrapped her sandwich. When she didn't pick it up to eat, but instead reached for a tube of applesauce for Lily, he reached over and whisked the baby out of Vanessa's lap. "I'll take care of her," he said. "You eat."

Around them, Christmas shoppers gathered at tables, drinking coffee and hot chocolate, showing each other their gift hauls. Jazzy Christmas carols could be heard in the background. The combined smell of coffee and old books filled the air.

Vanessa took a bite of sandwich, chewed, swallowed. It was egg salad, very mild, and it tasted good. She took another bite.

The urge to stop was there, but she reminded herself that it wasn't a healthy urge.

Gramma steadied her large sandwich with the fingers and thumb that stuck out of her wrist cast. "This is delicious," she said. "Way better than the cafeteria at the rehab."

"It *is* good," Vanessa agreed. She needed to recover, reduce stress, get strong. To do that, she needed to eat. She took another small bite.

And she needed to figure out what to do about Evan, how to handle this holiday season she'd committed to spending with this very stressful man.

Who was now watching her eat more closely than Snickers was.

After a few minutes of self-conscious nibbling, she'd had enough. In the past, she'd have hidden her irritation, stopped eating and found a way to conceal or throw away what was left on her plate. But she'd practiced ways to be more assertive throughout her therapy sessions, and it was time to use what she'd learned.

She put down her sandwich and glared at Evan. "Look. I'm going to be fine. I appreciate you and Gramma coming to my aid, but I need to handle my issues myself." She picked up her sandwich again and used it to point at Evan. "Don't you be watching me eat the way my brother does."

He huffed. "Fine. I'll finish eating and leave you two

in peace. I want to pick up a couple of books, anyway." He helped Lily eat a few more bites, scarfed down his own sandwich and headed over to the bookstore side of the shop.

Vanessa felt a different kind of empowerment than she'd felt last night and this morning. This time, it came from standing up for herself. Back when she and Evan had been together before, she hadn't stood up for herself; she'd just wallowed in letting Evan tell her what to do. He'd directed everything, and it hadn't been awful by any means, but it hadn't been the best way to start a relationship. She'd let her concerns build up inside and then bolted.

After they finished their lunch, they walked over to the bookstore side. Gramma moved well, if slowly, using a three-pronged cane with her good hand, stepping carefully with her boot-cast foot.

They browsed for a few minutes, navigating around people in the busy store. When they came to a more spacious area beside a tall shelf of thrillers, they both paused to look over the books. "You know," Gramma said suddenly, "I think you're going to do just fine. I liked how you spoke up to Evan just now. He cares, but he's a worrier, and he'd smother you if you let him."

The praise from Gramma surprised and pleased Vanessa. "I think you're right. I need to be strong on my own, not dependent on a man. Any man."

"Independence is good for you right now," Gramma said, "but when you're ready to get into a relationship with a man, Evan is a good one. You two were a wonderful couple."

Not exactly, Vanessa wanted to say but didn't. Not anymore, after life had happened and Vanessa had made choices of which Evan would definitely not approve.

Time for a change of subject. Vanessa turned toward a rack of Christmas trinkets.

"Oh, look at this," she said, holding up a red velvet headband, obviously made for little girls, decorated in white lace. "It would be perfect for Lily. I'm going to get it for her."

"You do that," Gramma said. "I'll be along as soon as I figure out which of this series I've read. They're all a bit alike." She propped her cane against the wall and picked up a thick political thriller while Vanessa continued to browse and then paid for the headband. She gently deflected the cashier from petting Snickers, explaining that a service dog needed to focus.

As Gramma paid for her things, Evan beckoned to Vanessa from a kids' play nook near the front windows. He sat on the edge of a chair, letting Lily crawl around, and of course, a couple of the nearby mothers were checking him out. He really was a good-looking guy. Put that together with being a nurturing father, and he was nearly irresistible.

But he wasn't for her.

She knelt down beside Lily, a safe distance from Evan's chair. "Thank you again for lunch," she said. "What's up?"

He used his foot to nudge a plastic truck into Lily's reach. "Look, uh, I wanted to say that I'm sorry I caused you stress."

"It's fine," she said. "It's me, not you. I'm easily stressed out. You've been very lenient with your nanny requirements."

He glanced around, clearly making sure that what he said next wouldn't be overheard. "I don't mean as an employer. I mean with the kissing. And how I acted afterward. I don't want to be any part of hurting you or causing you to backslide."

Her cheeks heated, and she glanced around to double-check that no one could overhear this too, too embarrassing conversation. But with the noise level in the shop, they had their privacy.

He went on. "I'm game to back entirely off the romance

thing. It's probably a good idea. But I'd still like to be your friend."

She met his eyes. "We tried that before. It didn't work."

"I know," he said, a smile tugging at the corner of his mouth. "I'm not saying it'll be easy, but let's try it again. We can make it work. And I really want to."

His concerned face was dear to her. "I want that, too," she said. She held out a hand. "Let's shake on it."

"Friends," he said.

"Friends," she agreed. And she wondered if that was really even a possibility, when the touch of his hand sent a rush of warmth to her heart.

On Thursday afternoon, Evan got home from a grocery run with Lily and found Declan sitting in the living room. He was tossing a ball from hand to hand and looking unhappy.

Even though Declan had only been home alone for a few minutes, Evan felt bad. He'd told Vanessa he could keep an eye on Declan until she got home. "Come help me put away these groceries," Evan said, "and tell me what's wrong." The boy had probably had an argument with a friend or gotten a poor grade on a test. Ten-year-old problems were still problems to the person who had them.

They put Lily into her jumpy seat in the kitchen doorway. Declan trudged back and forth bringing in the grocery haul, waving off Evan's suggestion that he put on a jacket. Every time Declan came through the back door with an armload of groceries, Lily jumped in the chair, her chubby little legs working, her arms pumping, a big smile on her face.

"She sure does like you," Evan said as he put oranges and salad vegetables into the fridge.

Instead of answering, Declan got down in Lily's face and blew a raspberry.

She laughed. "Deh! Deh!"

Evan tilted his head to one side, then walked over. "Hang on a minute," he said. "Lily, who's this?" He patted his own chest.

"Dah! Dah!"

"That's right," he said. He patted Declan's shoulder. "Who's this?"

"Deh! Deh!"

Declan's eyes widened. "She's saying my name!"

He nodded. "She sure is."

"She's smart! Aren't you?" Declan bounced her gently in the chair, making her laugh more.

Evan smiled and went back to putting groceries away. He didn't know much about children, but he was pretty sure that two of the sweetest ones were right here in this kitchen.

"Wonder when your mom will get home?" he asked when he'd finished. Vanessa had gone Christmas shopping with a friend this afternoon, and she'd asked Evan if he minded taking Lily for that part of the day, and then she'd watch Lily in the evening. He'd told her it was fine, and now he wanted to suggest that she take the evening off from the job, too. He was still concerned about her stress level and that he might contribute, somehow, to pushing her back into her eating disorder.

He'd actually caught himself watching her food consumption at a couple of meals recently. A glare from her had been enough to remind him that he wasn't to hover over her, that she could handle her problems herself.

Still, he cared. That was normal for a friend, right?

Silence from the kids made him look over. Declan had set the bouncy chair swinging, and Lily was falling asleep. Declan leaned against the wall and pulled his knees to his chest. He was staring off into space, looking sad again.

Evan washed his hands, then pulled out a chair at the kitchen table and sat down. "Your mom made cookies, it looks like."

"I'm not hungry," Declan said.

Evan blinked. If Declan wasn't hungry, things were serious. "Come on up here and tell me what's wrong." That was okay, right? If he was to be Vanessa's friend, it seemed okay for him to talk to her kid, find out what was bothering him.

Declan came to the table, sat down and started kicking the leg of the chair. "I spent all my money on a video game," he said, "and now I don't have anything for Christmas presents."

"Ah." He nodded. He had no idea how Vanessa handled Declan's money. At ten, Declan was too young to work, but he was old enough to have wants and needs. "You know, you don't need to get me or Lily anything. She's too little to notice, and I have everything I need."

"I wanna get Lily something. And I wanna get Mom something. But I can't."

"Hmm." Evan frowned. "Are you willing to do some chores for money?"

"Yeah!" Declan said. Then he deflated visibly. "Only Mom says I hafta do chores just because I'm part of the family, and I don't get paid for them."

"But these are extra," Evan said. "There's a woodpile in back of the house that's a big mess. It needs to be all stacked up neatly. It's a big job, and I don't have time to do it."

Declan brightened. "I can do that!"

"And I'd like some help cleaning out Gramma's guest room closet. If I stack up what goes to donations and what gets thrown away, I'd pay you to box them up and carry them out to the garage or the trash."

"Okay, yeah! Unless... Is that okay with Gramma Vi?"

"Believe it or not, she wants to get that done," he said.

"Let me text your mom and make sure this works for her. If it does, we've got a deal and you can earn some shopping money."

It *was* okay with Vanessa—she texted back, sure, thanks, with a smiley face—and Declan got started immediately. After Evan showed him how, he gamely put on work gloves and stacked wood, showing appropriate horror when they discovered a dead mouse at the edge of the pile. Seeing how quickly and competently the kid worked, Evan left him to it. He went inside and sorted the closet materials so Declan could come inside and start on that project.

After the chores were completed and money exchanged, Evan heated leftover macaroni and cheese for dinner, and they ate together with Lily. He wished Vanessa were there, he couldn't deny it. But he also knew it was better for them not to spend every moment at home together. And he enjoyed hearing Declan's stories of fourth-grade drama.

After dinner, they cleaned up together. "When Mom gets home, I'm gonna see if she'll take me shopping," Declan said. "She just can't see what I'm buying."

"She might be tired after spending the day out," Evan warned Declan.

His face fell. "Yeah. She probably will be."

Evan hesitated. "I have a few gifts to pick up," he said. "I was thinking of heading out to the mall later. If it's okay with your mom, you could come along."

Declan grabbed his coat. "Can we go now?"

A car door slammed outside. Vanessa. Evan couldn't help the very non-friend-like pounding of his heart.

Later, as they wandered through the shopping mall, Evan quickly realized that Declan had no idea of what to buy for his mother. They looked at various items, trying to decide. Slippers? Perfume? A sweater?

Finally, they called Gramma.

Of course, she had advice, and it made sense. "Get her something for Snickers," Gramma advised. "Also, her clothes are really casual, and she could use some nicer outfits. Date outfits."

Evan did not want to get Vanessa date clothes. He didn't want Vanessa to go out on dates, except with him.

Maybe he should ask Vanessa out on a date.

Except that wasn't being just friends. He had to be just friends with her, he reminded himself. Anything else would stress her out.

His own hesitations about being involved with her had been eclipsed by hers. For himself, he'd started to doubt his own perceptions that Vanessa was deceptive, an unreliable partner or even friend.

She was complicated. Just like anyone else. And he liked her, including her complications, enough to want to take things further.

Not if it would set her back emotionally, though. That was what it meant to truly care about someone, to be a good friend. You put their good over your own, even if that meant you couldn't get what you wanted.

He helped Declan pick out a sweater that would look good with her eyes. Not really date-like, but not *not* date-like. Then, while Declan talked to a friend, he slipped into a jewelry store and looked at necklaces and bracelets. But no. Jewelry was a girlfriend gift. She didn't want that.

"Can't decide?" the jeweler asked.

"Yeah, I don't really know what she likes."

"Women. They're all alike. They know exactly what they

want, but they won't tell you. They expect you to read their minds and get mad when you can't."

Whoa. That sounded personal. He gave the guy a sympathetic smile and nod. He'd been there, hurt by one woman and angry at all of them as a result.

Vanessa really wasn't like that. He was starting to understand that women were not all alike. They weren't all unreliable cheaters, like he had dedicated the past few years of his life to thinking. No, they were just varied, complex human beings, the same as men were.

Finally, he followed Gramma's advice and settled on a ridiculously expensive bright red collar for Snickers. He'd keep thinking about what he could get Vanessa, what would be right for a friend, and yet meaningful to her.

"Better get home," the pet store guy said as he rang up Evan's purchase. "Ice storm coming. We may shut down early."

"Mom hates winter storms," Declan said.

Uh-oh. Evan picked up the pace toward the exit. In the climate-controlled world of the mall, he hadn't realized it was getting bad outside.

He nearly slipped on an icy patch in the parking lot. "Text your mom and tell her we're on our way and we're fine," he told Declan.

He drove cautiously on the slushy, icy roads, the headlights barely piercing the sheets of freezing rain.

"Hey, Evan?" Declan said from the back seat. "You know how you paid me to do extra chores?"

"Uh-huh." Evan steered around a fallen tree branch.

"Well...if I did a lot of extra chores for you every week, do you think Mom and I could stay with you?"

Oh, wow. What to say. "Where you and your mom live is

an adult decision. You don't have to do chores to get to stay in a place you like, either."

"Okay." Declan sounded glum.

"But I'm glad you're a hard enough worker to suggest it."

"Thanks." As the car slid a little, Declan let out a little gasp. "I'll be glad when we get home."

So would Evan.

As he pulled into the driveway, the lit-up windows of Gramma's house gave him a sense of relief. Of happiness.

It was what he'd always felt when returning to this house, even as a child. Only now, it was intensified by his knowledge that Vanessa was inside, waiting for them.

He needed to slow down. He was feeling way too much for a friend.

Chapter Twelve

Relief washed over Vanessa when she saw the headlights of Evan's car. With Lily on her hip and Snickers at her side, she went to the front door.

They came up the porch steps, carrying shopping bags, Evan walking carefully and Declan slipping and sliding recklessly. She hugged Declan with her free arm, hesitated, and then hugged Evan, too. "I'm so glad you're home," she said. Her breathlessness had to do with how worried she'd been, not with hugging Evan. She was almost sure of it.

Wind gusted and icy rain fell. It was as if the sky was spitting slush. She closed the door, glad to have everyone at home.

There was a pop and an odd banging sound. The lights went out.

Snickers let out his high-pitched alarm bark.

"Whoa, what happened?" Declan asked.

Lily scrunched up her face and started the "uh-uh-uh" that meant she was about to cry.

Evan lifted Lily out of Vanessa's arms.

"Dah! Dah!" she cried.

"Let's see what's going on." Vanessa opened the door.

Evan wrapped the baby in a soft blanket, and they all went out onto the porch.

"Power's out up and down the street," Evan observed.

Voices came from the porch next door, and they walked out a little farther. "Anyone know what happened?"

"Probably a downed wire," a neighbor said.

Vanessa squinted over and spotted Mrs. Fenstermaker. "Everyone okay?" she called. Mrs. Fenstermaker was in her eighties and lived with her daughter and son-in-law.

"Fine, fine," the older woman called.

"Call or text if you need anything," Vanessa said.

"You, too," the son-in-law, Larry, said.

They went back inside, talking and exclaiming and taking off their jackets. "I'll find some candles," Vanessa said.

"Turn on your phone flashlight," Declan said.

"Don't use up your phone battery on the flashlight," Evan said. "Mine's charged, is yours?"

"Pretty good." She checked. "I'm on 65 percent."

They all moved into the kitchen. Vanessa quickly pulled a flashlight out of a drawer and handed it to Declan. "Hold it for me while I find candles," she said. "I think Gramma has a bunch of them somewhere."

"Bottom left cabinet," Evan said absently, which reminded her that this was his childhood home. He was swaying Lily back and forth while studying his phone. "Looks like there are outages everywhere. I'll report this one, but it may be a while before they get to us."

Declan opened the refrigerator and stood surveying its contents.

"No!" Vanessa said.

"Close it," Evan ordered at the same time.

Declan closed it, his brow wrinkling. "I'm just hungry."

"We have to be careful not to open it much," Vanessa explained. "We want to keep the cold inside so our food doesn't go bad."

"It's cold out here," Declan complained.

"It's because we had the door open. I'll turn up the heat."

"Furnace won't work," Evan said.

Vanessa stopped on her way to the thermostat, frowning. "But it's gas... Ohhhh."

"What?" Declan asked.

"Even gas furnaces use some electricity," she said. "Unfortunately, it's not going to work until the power comes back on. We may be in for a cold night." She frowned and looked at Evan. "Do you think we should try to find a hotel that has power?"

Evan shook his head. "The roads are already terrible."

"We almost went into a ditch!" Declan said.

"There's an old kerosene heater out in the garage, I think," Evan said. "But..."

Vanessa shook her head. "Too risky. You always read about fires that start from them." She located matches and started lighting candles, shivering. The temperature in the house couldn't have dropped that much, but the idea of being without heat made her feel cold, anyway.

"I stacked up the firewood earlier," Declan said. "Can we have a fire?"

"Of course! We should have thought of that. Good idea." She hugged him. "Thank you."

"Tell you what," Evan said. "Declan and I will bring in wood and get a fire started." He handed Lily back to her. "You'd better go drip water from a few faucets. We don't want to end up with frozen pipes."

"This is cool!" Declan said. He rushed out the kitchen door, leaving it wide-open.

Vanessa closed the door and glanced at Evan, wondering if Declan's mistakes would make him mad. He was, after all, a bit of a perfectionist.

But he was laughing. "Oh, to be ten again, when everything is an adventure." He went outside after Declan, closing the door behind him.

Snickers stayed close by her side while she walked around, setting faucets dripping and closing doors. Gramma's house was great, but it was old, with poorly insulated walls and windows. Better to keep the area near the fireplace as closed off as possible.

She had to admit to herself that it was nice to have Evan here to share responsibility for handling the storm and power outage.

She grabbed an armload of blankets from the linen cupboard and carried them down to the front room, where Evan was showing Declan how to build a fire. The sight of them kneeling together made Vanessa's heart squeeze.

Evan was so good for Declan. It was going to be hard on both of them when this period came to an end and they went their separate ways.

It was going to be hard on her, too. Melancholy threatened, but she shook it off much like Snickers shook himself after being out in the rain. She wasn't going to worry about tomorrow. *Each day has trouble enough of its own*, she reminded herself.

Soon, a fire flickered in the fireplace. Even though there was a screen in front of it, they all agreed to watch Lily carefully, to keep her from crawling too close. Even Snickers seemed in on the safety measure. He flopped down beside Lily, blocking her from the fire. She grabbed handfuls of his fur, then curled up beside him.

"Can we make s'mores?" Declan asked.

Vanessa shrugged. "Why not? Go get the supplies from the snack cupboard."

Evan smiled over at her. "I haven't had s'mores in years."

"They're just as good as ever," she said.

So they made s'mores and fed graham crackers to Lily—and a few bites to Snickers—and called Gramma Vi to make sure she was okay. She was; apparently the power was still on in the rehab center, and there were backup generators if it went out. She thanked them for taking care of her house and then ended the call in order to go back to her bridge game.

They told stories of past snow- and ice storms. This area of the Eastern Shore didn't get a lot of snow, but ice was a problem.

Evan kept checking the weather. "It's not going to let up for a while," he said. "Roads are getting worse and lots of people are without electricity." He scrolled further. "Power company estimates that it could be twenty-four to forty-eight hours before they can restore power."

"Wow."

She looked over at Declan. He'd curled up behind Lily, who was next to Snickers, and his eyes were sleepy.

"You realize we're all going to have to sleep down here," Evan commented.

"Cool," Declan said, sounding half asleep. "Can you get me a pillow, Mom?"

"I'll get us all pillows." It would give her a chance to cool off from the thought of spending the night in the same room as Evan.

When she came back in, he'd added more wood to the fire and was replacing the screen. "I'll wake up every couple of hours and keep this going," he said.

"We can take turns," she said.

"No. You sleep. I'll do it." His eyes were warm on her. "Gentleman's duty."

She smiled, feeling her face heat. She had to admit that she liked his protectiveness.

They were safe. All of them: her, and Snickers, and the kids. And Evan.

But Vanessa's heart was another story. It didn't feel safe at all.

Throughout the night, Evan slept fitfully. He'd set his phone alarm to go off every two hours, but he woke up before it went off every time. He didn't want to wake up Lily. Didn't want to wake up Vanessa, either. They both needed their sleep.

Besides, he liked watching Vanessa sleep. She lay on her side, like a child, at the feet of the actual children. Her hair spread out over her pillow, and her cheeks were flushed pink. Her breathing was even.

All he wanted in the world was to keep her, and the children, safe.

It was a confusing feeling. He'd decided when his wife left that he didn't want to risk it with women again. When he'd learned he was a father, he'd gotten even more determined to guard his heart. Now, it wasn't just his emotional state that was at risk, it was his daughter's well-being.

Vanessa was proving herself to be a different person from the one he'd thought he knew twelve years ago. Maybe it was motherhood that had changed her. Or maybe he'd been looking at things wrong.

Maybe he could make something work between them. Friendship, sure, but that wasn't all he wanted. He wanted the whole package.

Fear held him back. What if he pursued it, like he had before, and she blithely rejected him? He remembered the shock and pain of that as if it were yesterday.

It wouldn't be shocking a second time. He knew it could happen. It had already happened, that day in church when she'd told him they needed to keep a professional distance between them.

That idea didn't seem to be sticking. But the ups and downs of their connection felt more painful now than when they were younger.

Back then, he'd been young and inexperienced, honestly more aware of his physical desire for Vanessa than of anything deeper. His pain had come as much from hurt pride and anger as from a broken heart.

Now, he'd seen Vanessa caring for her son and for his daughter. He'd shared meals with her and gotten her help with Lily. She'd been the one to spot Lily's delays before he'd done so. Just now, she'd been a true partner in dealing with this minor weather disaster.

He wanted a true partner. Wanted that emotional connection even more than he wanted to hold her in his arms, although that desire was there, too.

Lily shifted and let out a sigh, and he scooted over to pull a blanket back over her where she'd kicked it away. He smoothed down her hair and watched her breathe.

She was his priority. She had to be.

Declan, though, was a great kid. Evan wouldn't mind staying involved in his life. To his own surprise, the boy seemed to look up to him, to want to spend time with him, to listen when he spoke.

Evan was just a geeky engineer who'd never contemplated being a father figure. But he found he didn't mind the idea with Declan.

And it was a delight to watch Declan and Lily interact together. Lily seemed to sense, instinctively, that Declan was a different kind of being than her father or even Vanessa. Lily leaned on the adults, turned to them when she was sad or hungry or tired. But it was Declan who lit her up with joy.

Taking Lily away from Vanessa and Declan would hurt her, he could see that. In this short time since Thanksgiving, she'd become attached to them.

He lay back and stared at the ceiling, in the flickering firelight. He started to doze off.

Flickering. Flickering. More flickering.

He sat upright. Something was wrong. He looked over at the fireplace, his heart racing. But the fire burned low and safe behind its screen.

Vanessa and Declan and Lily and Snickers slept on, but that flickering... He stood and went to the window.

Fire shot out of the window next door.

"Wake up!" Evan shouted. He stepped past Declan and shook Vanessa's shoulder. "Call the fire department. Fire at the Fenstermakers' house." He ran to the door and stuck his feet into boots.

"Declan, get the fire extinguisher and take it next door," he heard Vanessa call as he sped toward the neighbors' house.

He could see flames flickering through the Fenstermakers' sliding glass door. He pounded on it, yelling. When there was no response, he ran to the front door and pounded there, ringing the doorbell and yelling.

The son-in-law flung open the door. He looked disoriented.

"Fire in your back room." Evan opened the screen door himself and shoved past the man. "Get everyone out. Pets, too."

He rushed through the house toward the pungent, oily smell. Beside the sliding doors, a small kerosene heater was in flames. Impossible to turn the thing off now. He spotted a blanket and tried to remember whether that was the right way to extinguish an oil fire.

"Here!" Declan rushed to his side and thrust a red fire extinguisher into his hands.

He grabbed it. "Go outside," he ordered. "Leave the door open." Behind Declan, he could see old Mrs. Fenstermaker being guided downstairs by her daughter.

Evan pulled the pin, aimed the extinguisher nozzle low and squeezed the handle. He swept the nozzle back and forth. Within seconds, the fire was out.

"I've got water!" The son-in-law came rushing in with a bucket.

"It's out." Evan was hyped with adrenaline. "Let's keep an eye on it, in case it reignites."

"Thanks, man. I'll watch it. Everyone's safe."

After calling the fire department back to let them know the danger was past, Evan walked outside. Only when he raked a hand through his hair did he realize he had a burn across his knuckles.

Mrs. Fenstermaker and her daughter were on the front walkway, wrapped in blankets, arguing. "I told you that thing was dangerous," Mrs. Fenstermaker was saying.

"I *know*, Mom. Can you stop?"

Vanessa came out on the front steps of Gramma's house, Lily on one hip. "Everyone okay?" she called. "We have a fire and blankets if you need to get warm."

It was getting light, the sky turning to pale gray. A neighbor from across the street walked over and stood chatting with the son-in-law. A car stopped to see what was going on.

Mrs. Fenstermaker's daughter came over to him. "Thank you *so* much," she said, giving him a quick hug. "You probably saved our lives."

A few more neighbors came out. As the sun rose, someone brought out a camp stove and made coffee. Then the neighbor on the other side made a fire in their firepit, and everyone drifted over to drink coffee and talk about how they'd handled the night and when the power might come back on. Declan and a couple of other kids started running and sliding on the ice.

All the adrenaline was leaving Evan's body, and he sat down on a picnic bench. He watched everyone enjoying the fire's warmth and the promise of a sunny day. Vanessa sat on the porch steps with Lily, and Declan stopped playing periodically to come over and talk to Lily and tickle her, each time earning a big laugh and a "Deh! Deh!"

"That Declan is such a nice boy," Mrs. Fenstermaker said, sitting down beside Evan. "Takes after his mother, not his father."

Another neighbor sat down across the table. "Who is his father, anyway? I heard it was Oscar Anderson."

Evan went alert, listening for Mrs. Fenstermaker's denial.

It didn't come.

No way could Declan's father be Oscar Anderson. Angie's late husband? Who'd been married to Angie until his death a few years ago?

"Vanessa's such a sweet girl now," the gossipy neighbor said. "You'd never guess that she...did that."

"People can change," Mrs. Fenstermaker said firmly.

Evan excused himself and backed away slowly as the two women went on talking.

He stared at Vanessa. She looked so pretty and sweet, walking around with a coffeepot now, smiling and laughing.

She *looked* sweet. Way too sweet to have been with a married man. But the neighbor had sounded certain. Was it possible? Could all that goodness be a facade?

Could Vanessa be a cheater who broke up families, just like Evan's mother had been?

When Vanessa handed off Lily to Declan and went inside, he followed her.

"Hey, good job, hero man," she said, smiling at him.

He ignored the compliment. "I just heard something," he said. "One of the neighbors mentioned who Declan's father was. Is it true that you were with Oscar Anderson? While he was married to Angie?"

She stared at him, her eyes wide. Then she glanced around, looked out the window. She turned back. "Yes. It's a whole long story, but yes."

The electricity came back on, signaled by the whirrs and beeps of appliances and the too-bright kitchen light.

There was a part of him that had hoped he was wrong. So much so that he felt himself deflate like a leaky tire. "I'll take care of Lily today," he said abruptly. "I don't even want to look at you." Then he turned on his heel and left the house.

Chapter Thirteen

Vanessa stared after Evan as he slammed his way outside.

For just a second, her world froze. She couldn't breathe. And then she did suck in a breath, and the ache inside her went from her throat to her stomach, making her cringe in on herself. She crossed her arms over her chest, her shoulders hunching.

She'd wondered how he would react if and when he learned of Declan's parentage. Had figured that his upright, moral streak would recoil from it. Understandably so.

She'd been right. And being right had never felt so wrong in her life.

Without knowing more than a little neighborhood gossip about her story, he'd decided that she was bad and wrong. That he didn't want her caring for Lily. That he didn't even want to look at her.

She turned to the window and watched as he took Lily back from Declan. He wasn't even wearing a jacket, just a down vest over a Henley. The same shirt he'd slept in, actually. She was wearing those same clothes, too, and it looked like all the neighbors were as well. She spied lots of puffy jackets layered over plaid flannel pants.

Evan appeared to want to turn away from the crowd—she could read him pretty well by now—but everyone kept coming up to him, talking to him, pounding him on the back. He was the hero of the day. Mrs. Fenstermaker had told her she felt Evan had saved her life, and it was probably true.

He was a great guy. Heroic. Protective. She'd known it from the first time she met him. She'd been stumbling drunk out of a bar, and he'd stopped and helped her, taken her to the emergency room for her broken wrist, brought her back to his grandmother's house. This very house. He'd just meant for her to have a meal and sleep off the hangover, but at Gramma's, and then Evan's, insistence, she'd ended up staying.

She'd known it couldn't work long-term, though. Not with the differences in their values and lifestyles.

For all her foolish behavior, she'd been smarter back then.

Now, she was breathless with the hurt of what he'd said, because she'd let herself care. Let herself laugh with him, and cook for him, and take care of his child. Let herself fantasize that last night was how it would be, she and Declan with Evan and Lily, cuddled up around the hearth, making s'mores.

She looked out the window again. Declan was talking earnestly to Evan. The hero worship was evident in his stance and his expression.

The worst of it was that Declan had given a little bit of his heart to Evan, too. That would make it bad when they all parted ways.

She watched them talk and a sudden fear gripped her. Declan. Would Evan push his negative views about her, and Oscar, onto Declan?

For her son's sake, she had to deal with this crisis properly and well. But how? What should she do first?

Her heart raced, too hard. Close to a panic attack. She clung to the edge of the kitchen sink, bent over it, her chest heaving.

There was a nudge at her knees. Snickers.

She sank down onto the floor and buried her head in Snickers's thick coat. The dog licked her and climbed halfway into her lap.

Deep breaths, deep breaths. Gradually, her heart rate went back down. Maybe not to a normal level, but to a less scary level, anyway.

The cabinets against her back held her up. The old linoleum floor was cold beneath her, but Snickers was warm. The furnace had kicked on, too. Soon the whole house would be warm, everyone's would. Neighbors would quit hanging around outside and return to their homes.

How were she and Evan going to manage living in this house together now? Would he want her to move?

She petted Snickers's head, trying to keep her breathing steady.

This feeling, of not being good enough, was all too familiar. Images flashed through her head like a slideshow. High school, when she was a little too chubby and her clothes came from the thrift store. She'd thought getting skinny would help, and in a certain sense, it had. Boys had stopped making fun of her and started asking her out. But something about her seemed to tell them not to take her seriously. She'd been tossed aside a few times, for classier, wealthier girls.

And then she'd made a decision that seemed logical at the time. If men were going to take advantage of her, she was going to get something back. She'd found girlfriends with similar attitudes and started driving into the city, frequenting high-end clubs and bars where wealthy businessmen hung out after their workdays were done. She'd always, always checked for a wedding ring before letting things go beyond a little joking around and the purchase of a drink or two.

But some men, like Oscar, didn't wear wedding rings

even though they were married. She'd only learned of Angie's existence when she'd called Oscar to let him know she'd gotten pregnant.

She scratched Snickers's ears, remembering that dark time. She'd tried hard to keep herself healthy during the pregnancy, but it hadn't been easy, losing her figure, feeling fat again, fat and alone. She'd adored Declan from the moment she laid eyes on him, all red and wrinkly and squalling. But still, she'd periodically freaked out and gone down the rabbit hole of anorexia. Her brother had come home from his stint in the military just in time to help her out, taking Declan when she wasn't doing well at caring for him.

Lately, she'd been getting so much better. Therapy had made a difference. Snickers even more of one. A good church home and new friends had built her up most of all.

That was probably why she'd made the mistake of thinking she just might, possibly, be able to have it all, including a relationship with a good man like Evan.

But no. He'd learned the truth about her and ripped her heart out of her chest.

"Mom?" Declan came into the kitchen and then rushed to her. "Are you okay?"

He sounded scared, and who could blame him? He'd seen her fall apart before, seen her pass out on the floor even, called Luke or 911 for help. She could hear in his voice that he feared those days were back again.

That couldn't happen. She had to be strong for her son. She straightened her spine. "I'm fine," she said, hugging Declan. "Just a little tired. And I need to talk to Evan. Could you take care of Lily for ten or fifteen minutes, over at the Fenstermakers' house?"

"Sure," he said, hugging her back.

She stroked his hair. "You did a really good job today, taking that fire extinguisher over so quickly."

He blushed and ducked his head. "I love you, Mom," he said, his voice low and husky. And then he jumped up and ran outside. "Evan!" he yelled at the top of his lungs. "Mom wants to talk to you!"

Embarrassing, but the public nature of the request might make Evan actually comply. Vanessa stood quickly and splashed cold water on her face, then dried it with paper towels.

Evan came in, barely. He leaned against the wall beside the door and crossed his arms. "What?"

He was so handsome that it hurt to look at him. What hurt more was that they'd descended so quickly to the angry "what" in response to a request to talk.

She touched Snickers's head for reassurance, and the big dog leaned against her.

Don't break down. This is for Declan. She crossed her arms, mimicking his closed posture. "I wanted to make sure you didn't say anything negative to Declan about...what you found out today."

His mouth twisted a little. "I won't. I care about him. I try not to hurt people I care about."

Okay, Mr. Superior. "I thought you cared about me, and yet you don't seem to have any problem hurting me."

Something flickered across his face, but so quickly that she couldn't read it. "You're not who I thought you were. I would never have expected you to..." He puffed out a disgusted breath and looked away.

"You're aware that you don't know the whole story, correct?"

"I know enough." His lip curled.

Heat flashed through her body. "Do you? I thought you scientific types liked actual evidence."

"We do. Exhibit A just came out to tell me you wanted to talk."

She sucked in a breath and let it out, slowly. She could hear neighbors calling out goodbyes. Out the window, she saw a couple of dads putting out the bonfire. She stroked Snickers's soft head, over and over.

If Evan was going to call Declan's very existence evidence of her shameful wrongdoing, there was no arguing with him. She'd felt that shame herself, early on. It had taken a lot of prayer and Bible reading to convince herself that she wasn't irredeemable. No one was.

She hadn't known Oscar was married. Okay. But if she'd been living right, she wouldn't have been out trying to meet rich guys in the first place, let alone going back to their hotel rooms.

God had forgiven her, and because of that, she was well on the road to forgiving herself. Proof that He turned everything to good was Declan himself, her kind, funny, intelligent son.

She lifted her chin and glared at Evan. "Just promise me you'll avoid hurting Declan as much as you can. It's his father we're talking about, and I try never to be negative. He's too young to understand the situation that led to his conception."

"He certainly is. I won't speak of it to him."

"We can retreat to our own sides of the house," she said, "since you can't stand to look at a sinner like me."

His brows pulled in. "I thought you were different."

"I'm definitely different from perfect people like you who never make mistakes." She paused and propped a hand on her hip. "I've made plenty. But I hope I've never rejected someone based on a few lines of neighborhood gossip."

"I came to you to find out if it was true."

"It *is* true. I was stupid and sinful and wrong, okay? But I'm learning to forgive myself, because I'm forgiven in Christ. Read your Bible, Evan."

He made a growling sound in his throat.

"Do you want me to continue taking care of Lily? Or do you think I'll contaminate her with my lack of morals?"

"I'll text you," he said and banged his way out the door.

The lights flickered out, then came back on. The few people who were left outside exclaimed and cheered.

Vanessa knelt beside Snickers again, taking deep breaths. She *would* get through this. But whether Evan decided she should continue working for him or not, the next few weeks weren't going to be easy. Was she strong enough to deal with them?

She had her doubts, but for her son's sake, she had to try.

Neither Evan nor Lily slept well on Friday night, and it showed on Saturday morning. They were both cranky as Evan prepared breakfast. Neither of them ate much.

Evan had one ear cocked toward Vanessa's side of the house. He half expected her to come in and criticize him again for having morals. But although he could hear movement, he didn't see Vanessa, Declan or Snickers.

Which was fine. He was still furious with her for pretending to be a decent human being when she was anything but.

He was furious at himself, too. How had he let himself get so enmeshed in Vanessa's life, so hopeful about a future with her? How had he forgotten that she'd dumped him before?

Well, now he'd dumped her back. But that awareness was anything but satisfying.

He decided to clean house today. Christmas was coming and Gramma would be staying here for several days, and he wanted to make sure the place was up to her high standards of housekeeping. He got out the vacuum cleaner and dust cloths and went into the living room.

Lily crawled after him, and he realized he'd need to put her in her playpen if he meant to get anything done. He dragged it in and plunked her inside with her stacking rings and a stuffed tiger.

She wasn't having it. She lifted her arms to him and cried, "Dah! Dah!" until he relented and picked her up.

There was a baby carrier Vanessa used sometimes, a sort of backpack except it faced front. He located it while Lily alternated between crying and crawling toward everything dangerous.

Vanessa had mentioned doing more childproofing, since Lily was rapidly getting more mobile, but they hadn't taken action. Now, he'd have to do it alone.

Fighting off the blues, he adjusted the baby carrier to his larger frame and eased Lily into it. After a couple of minutes, she settled down. There. He was doing fine. He had this down.

He sprayed furniture dusting spray on a microfiber cloth and went around the room dusting. Lily looked on with interest as he picked up statues and framed photos, dusting them off.

They weren't too bad. Vanessa must have dusted in here recently.

She was great at her job. More than a nanny, she'd become an important part of his life and a crucial part of Lily's. He couldn't fathom managing everything alone, now that he'd come to understand what was involved in caring for a baby.

The idea of finding another nanny after the holidays was repugnant to him. He didn't want anyone else living in his home, learning his routines, figuring out what Lily liked and needed.

So he'd find a nanny who didn't live in. Or maybe a great day care. Vanessa would know—

No. He couldn't consult Vanessa. He needed to stop relying on her if he was going to let her go.

"Hey, Evan, want to go ice sledding?" Declan's exuberant voice sounded from the kitchen. "Where are you guys?"

The sight of the ten-year-old filled Evan with a sense of loss. "I can't go," he said sharply. Then, instantly, he regretted his tone. "I have some other stuff to do," he said.

"Okay." Declan shrugged and left. Minutes later, the back door slammed. Evan couldn't help watching him out the window.

Declan joined up with a friend from the neighborhood. They walked alongside a man who couldn't be anything other than the boy's father. Their identical heads of red hair made that clear.

He felt a sudden sadness for Declan, who'd never have a father he could go ice sledding with. He recognized that one edge of the sadness was for himself. He'd never had a father to do the guy stuff with him, either.

Evan would have liked to go with Declan today. Would have liked to learn what ice sledding was. To spend that time with Declan, to provide the boy with a male role model or at least a friend. Vanessa would have been glad to take care of Lily while they did that. In fact, she'd have probably had hot chocolate waiting for them when they came home.

In so many ways she was a good woman.

He doubled down on his cleaning, running the vacuum and then tackling a stack of papers that had piled up on the shelf by the door. Lily was surprisingly cooperative; she actually fell asleep in the carrier despite the noise he was making.

He couldn't push Vanessa out of his mind. How had she gotten involved with a married man? He knew she'd lived more wildly back then, but it still seemed beyond the silly shenanigans he'd known about. She could have broken up a marriage, just like his mother had broken up their family.

He started thinking about Oscar. You couldn't just blame the woman in a situation like this. Oscar must have been a fully cooperating participant. In fact, he'd probably initiated things.

Vanessa had said he didn't know the whole story. Well, undoubtedly there was a story. He just couldn't have any way of knowing what parts of it were true. Because to participate in an adulterous affair, you had to do a lot of lying. Vanessa must be very skilled at it, because he'd not had a clue.

He went out to the kitchen to get a drink and found Snickers lounging on his side. When the dog heard him, he lumbered to his feet and came over, tail wagging.

"Doh-ee," Lily said, pointing. "Doh-ee."

"Yes, that's a doggy!" Evan's heart raced with excitement. Another new word. He opened his mouth to call for Vanessa and then shut it again. They weren't on "share happy news about the baby" terms, not anymore.

He knelt and rubbed Snickers's ears while Lily chanted "Doh-ee" several more times, reaching for Snickers, and he let her touch the dog, careful to pull her hands away before she could squeeze and hold on.

He heard Vanessa moving around and craved to see her. Ironic since he'd told her, in what was admittedly a cruel way, that he couldn't stand to look at her.

He couldn't stand not to, either.

Impatient with himself, he bundled Lily into her jacket, hat and mittens. He grabbed his own coat and boots, and they headed for the library.

On such a sunny Saturday, the place was doing a brisk

business. He walked in and one of the librarians greeted him. "Are you here for story time?" he asked.

"I think she's a little young for that," he said, shifting Lily from one side to the other. She was getting heavy, and wiggly, too.

"Not at all," the librarian said. "It's baby story time today, for little ones from birth to eighteen months. Board books and rhymes and singing. She'll love it, won't you, sweetie?" He clucked at Lily.

Lily immediately went into a string of babbling, talking back to the man, and Evan laughed and took her upstairs to the children's section.

He may as well do this as anything else.

He wasn't sure why he should feel so depressed when he'd done the right thing. When he was in the right. After all, *he* wasn't the one who'd had an affair with a married person, like Vanessa. *He* wasn't the one who'd neglected to tell an ex that they had a baby together, like his wife. *He* wasn't the one who'd dumped a child on his grandmother so that said child wouldn't interfere with an exciting lifestyle, like his mother.

In a room off the main children's book area, he saw a circle of parents and babies. A cheerful-looking woman was unpacking a bag of board books and baby toys, clearly preparing to take the lead.

"Evan. Over here." There was Luke with the toddler Lily had played with at their house. "Glad to see you, man. I thought I might be the only dad here."

"I got roped in by the librarian. Nothing else to do today."

They chatted for a few minutes and then joined the others in chanting with their babies, clapping their hands together, waving their kids' fingers, singing little songs. Evan felt ridiculous, but he pushed forward with it. Lily was wide-eyed, watching the other babies and, at times, trying to imitate them.

Evan could see that activities like this would be good for Lily's verbal abilities. Probably her physical ones, too, since tapping and kicking and clapping were part of what the early intervention specialist had recommended on her last visit.

As the extremely energetic group leader directed their activities, Evan watched Luke participate with apparent comfort. The man seemed at peace. Evan wished he had that for himself, but he had to acknowledge that he didn't.

It struck him that Luke, being Vanessa's brother, probably knew about Declan's father. In fact—he was putting it together now—Luke was married to Angie, who must have found out the painful truth about her husband's cheating, too. If Gramma's neighbors knew, then Luke and Angie, much more closely connected, must know as well.

For that matter, if Gramma's neighbor knew, then did Gramma know? After all, she'd hired Vanessa as her companion and caregiver.

But no, he remembered, Gramma had asked him whether *he* was Declan's father.

So everyone didn't know, but some did. And those who knew had apparently overlooked Vanessa's behavior. More than overlooked; they must have forgiven it.

Was he the one who was wrong, then, for being offended by what she'd done? By finding that it put her character so much into question that he couldn't handle being around her, nor leaving his child with her?

Maybe so. But Evan knew from a child's point of view what happened when families were torn up by adultery.

So should he allow Vanessa to continue living in and being a nanny? Would she even want to after what he'd said to her?

"Waah!" Lily suddenly burst out crying, her face red. A

moment later, she spit up onto the leg of Evan's jeans, herself and the floor.

Evan was paralyzed by embarrassment and concern.

Luke handed Evan a burp cloth. "Happens to all of us, man," he said.

The perky leader grabbed a container of antibacterial wipes and tossed it their way like a football. Luke caught it, pulled out a couple of wipes and cleaned up the floor.

The program continued on. None of the other parents seemed bothered by what had happened.

Evan used the burp cloth to wipe off himself and Lily as best he could. "Thanks for the help, man," he said to Luke. "I'd better get her home." He gathered up Lily and her diaper bag, waved to the room generally and left.

As he put Lily into her car seat, he held a hand to her forehead. She seemed warm, but no more than other times, or at least he didn't think so. But she was crying and red-faced and clearly uncomfortable.

He'd take her home, give her a light lunch if she wanted it and put her down for her nap. Hopefully, that would make her feel better, because if it didn't, he had no idea of what to do.

Chapter Fourteen

At 4:00 a.m. Sunday morning, Evan heard a strange sound and sat upright in bed. Something was wrong.

He rushed through the open door to Lily's crib.

She was crying a fussy, low-pitched cry, almost a bleat. Her eyes were closed, her breathing labored. When he touched her, she felt hot.

He stroked her arm, his heart pounding, trying to think of what to do.

Should he take her to the ER? That was probably the only option at this hour. But the thought of a long wait, of Lily's fear and discomfort, of how she'd feel poked and prodded by strange doctors... No. His barely sprouted parental instincts told him that wasn't the right move.

He knew what he wanted to do. What he had to do. He wiped her forehead, made sure she was safe in her crib and then trotted upstairs. He tapped on Vanessa's door.

There was no response, so he tapped again. This time, he heard movement, and then she came to the door. Her hair was loose and disheveled, and she wore a T-shirt and shorts.

"Evan? What's wrong?" She squinted at him.

"Lily is sick and I don't know what to do." He held his breath. Would she reject his request? She had every right to do so, given how he'd acted toward her. "I don't know if it's serious enough for the ER or not. Would you mind taking a look at her?"

"Of course, I'll come." She grabbed a hoodie and pulled it on, then followed him downstairs and through the chilly, moonlit house to Lily's room.

On the way, he explained what he'd seen so far. When they got to the room, Lily was crying louder than she had been before.

Vanessa hurried to Lily, felt her forehead, and then picked her up. "She does feel warm. Did you take her temperature?"

"I don't think I have a thermometer," he said, feeling ashamed.

"Go look in the medicine closet in the hall bathroom. I think Gramma has a thermometer there. I've used it for Declan before."

"Okay." He rushed out, found a digital thermometer and hurried back.

Vanessa had taken Lily's shirt off, and the baby was wailing. Vanessa held out her hand for the thermometer, then tucked it into Lily's armpit and held her arm against her side. "Try to quiet her down," she mouthed over Lily's cries. "I can't hear the beep."

Evan found Lily's stuffed crab and waved it in front of her, made it tickle her. Her cries slowed down, and there was the thermometer's beep-beep-beep.

Vanessa squinted at the thermometer. "One hundred point eight," she said.

"Is that bad?" he asked.

"Not terrible, I don't think," she said. "Look it up on your phone."

He hadn't even thought of that. Where was his brain? He rushed into his bedroom and got his phone, then went back into Lily's room. Vanessa was in the rocking chair talking and humming and rocking, but Lily still fussed and twisted, obviously uncomfortable.

Evan ached to see it. He wished he could take on her discomfort for himself. He searched "how high is bad for baby temp" and the list of results as well as variations on the wording was a little bit reassuring. He wasn't the only one referring to Dr. Google in the middle of the night.

He found a site and read the answer, then reinforced it with another. "Anything over ninety-nine is considered a fever for an armpit temperature. But..." He trailed off and continued searching. "You should take your toddler to the ER if their temperature is above 102," he said. "So that answers that. But what do I do now?"

"I always used to use cool washcloths with Declan," she said, still rocking. "Why don't you go get a couple? It might make her feel better."

What made *him* feel better was having someone else there with whom to share his concern. He had a brief flash of insight: what it must have been like for Vanessa to raise Declan alone, to face this sort of worry as a first-time mom with no partner or relative to help.

He wetted a couple of washcloths in the bathroom, squeezed them out and hurried back.

"Wipe her face with one," Vanessa coached. "Actually, here, you hold her." She vacated the rocker and nodded toward it. He sat, and she put Lily into his arms.

He braced himself for an outcry, but Lily actually quieted a little in his arms. That pleased him. He wiped her red face and then patted the wet cloth on her bare arms.

"There. See? That comforts her." Vanessa frowned. "Do you have any baby fever medicine?"

He shook his head. Why didn't he? "I should have picked

some up yesterday, when she was a little stuffed up, but I didn't."

"Then I'm guessing you don't have a syringe to suction her nose, either."

He couldn't help making a face. "I have to do that?"

She laughed. "I mean, sometimes it can help, as I recall."

"I don't even have a pediatrician for her. I feel like a loser of a father."

Vanessa shook her head. "Don't beat yourself up," she said. "You're just learning, and anyway, nobody really knows how to be a parent. You're kind of winging it the whole time, I'm sorry to tell you."

As they spoke, he kept gently wiping Lily's face and rocking her, and her cries were settling down. Every few minutes, she'd have trouble catching her breath and snort.

"I'm trying to think of somebody who'd be up now and willing to give us, or get us, some medicine for her fever," he said.

"I'll text Luke. He's always up early."

She did, and then they took turns holding and comforting Lily. Thirty minutes later, there was a tap at the front door. To Evan's surprise, it wasn't Luke, but Angie. She handed him a bag with medicine and other items. "I hope this helps," she said. "I can't stay, our little one is sick, too, but call if you need anything and one of us will help."

Evan winced. "I hope Lily didn't pass along whatever she has."

"Oh, all the kids are getting sick at this time of year. Who knows who gave what to whom?"

Vanessa appeared at the doorway to his suite, Lily in her arms. "Hey, Angie, do you know how long whatever this is, is supposed to last?"

"Maisey Sherman says it's a twenty-four hour thing," Angie said. "I hope she's right."

They thanked her profusely, then settled in the living room with the baby. Vanessa held her while Luke read the instructions on the medicine. Vanessa showed him how to fill the dropper and make sure she ingested it rather than spitting it out. The process made her cry again, but soon she settled down. Ten minutes later, she drifted off to sleep.

Light was coming through the windows now, a beautiful pink-tinged sunrise visible through skeletal trees. A car drove by. Lily felt solid in his arms, a weight pushing him down to earth, reminding him of what was important.

She was important. The most important thing.

He was starting to doubt that he could do this alone, which was, after all, why he'd come to Gramma's in the first place. But tonight, it wasn't Gramma who'd helped him, it was Vanessa. Her wisdom and knowledge were a boon to him.

He looked at her makeup-free face, her forehead wrinkling as she tried to find an old movie on TV. Her hair was spread out on her shoulders, and her feet were pulled up under her. She looked impossibly young.

Impossibly beautiful.

And he didn't need to be thinking that kind of thought about Lily's nanny, the woman who'd caused him pain before, the woman whose moral standards he'd discovered to be way lower than they should be.

Lily was sleeping now, breathing more easily, no doubt a result of the medicine. He leaned back, his eyes starting to close.

He snapped awake when Vanessa lifted Lily out of his arms. "You should go get some sleep," she said. "I don't mind staying with her for a little while."

"No, you should." He met her eyes. "I'm very grateful you were willing to help despite...everything."

"Of course," she said. "I'm not a monster, Evan. I love this little sweetie." She kissed the top of Lily's head.

He watched them for a minute, his heart full. Then he grabbed an energy drink from the fridge. "You want one?" he called from the kitchen doorway, holding it up.

"No way," she said.

He chugged the drink and then took the baby from her. He expected her to leave, to go back to bed, but she stayed.

As the sun rose, she started texting other moms she knew. After a few responses pinged in, she looked up. "Everyone says what Angie said, that it's a twenty-four-hour bug. Which is good, since Christmas is coming."

"I think she's cooling down already," Evan said. Lily was sleeping in his arms.

"Good." She smiled at him.

He smiled back, let his gaze linger.

Her forehead wrinkled, and she looked away as if she had just remembered their fight. "Actually, I think I'll go grab another hour or two of sleep before church," she said, "if you're okay."

"I'm okay. Thank you, Vanessa. I mean it."

"You're welcome." She turned and walked quickly upstairs.

Who could blame her for being guarded? He felt guarded himself and confused. Was Vanessa the horrible person he'd pegged her for upon hearing about Declan's father? Or was she the kind, gentle person who'd taken loving care of Lily for the past three, almost four weeks, and who'd readily gotten up in the night to help care for her?

Evan had always liked questions with one right answer. He thought in black and white, not in shades of gray.

But nothing was black and white now, in parenting or in life.

***

On Monday, Vanessa woke up feeling good. She'd mostly recovered from the lack of sleep Saturday night, or rather, early Sunday morning. She'd continued to help Evan care for Lily all day yesterday, and the baby was definitely on the mend.

Her relationship with Evan might be on the mend, too.

There had been no more of that "I don't want to look at you" negative attitude. He'd expressed real appreciation for her help, and she'd felt good that she could help Lily and also help Evan learn to be a father. She loved being useful, and she'd definitely felt needed.

Today was Declan's first day of Christmas vacation, and he celebrated by sleeping in and then playing video games all morning. After lunch, she decided they needed to do something a little more constructive. Evan was out: he'd taken Lily to a new pediatrician who came highly recommended, just to check her over and assure himself that she was really okay.

"We can make Christmas cookies or salt dough ornaments," she told her son. "You choose, and then we'll take them to our friends and neighbors as gifts."

"Cookies!" Declan said. "Can I decorate them?"

"We'll do some frosted sugar cookies, so yes, you can decorate those," she said. They'd be messy looking rather than artistic, but that was fine. Their friends would appreciate the effort. She decided she'd make peanut blossoms, too—Declan could unwrap chocolate candies and put them on top of the peanut butter cookies. And they'd make fudge. That would take all afternoon, but she didn't mind.

And sure, in her heart she looked forward to Evan's expression when he came back to a house that smelled delicious, like a home.

They were rolling out dough and cutting it into shapes

with Gramma Vi's old cookie cutters when Declan said, "Mom?"

"What?" She gathered the scraps of dough from the table and rolled them into a ball.

"Do you think we can stay here, in this house?" His tone was plaintive.

"You really want to, don't you?"

"Yeah. I want to stay at my same school and on the same street with Jason and Pete. And I like this house. And Gramma Vi." He hesitated. "And Evan and Lily, too."

Vanessa drew in her breath slowly, held it for a few seconds, then let it out. "I just don't know, kiddo," she said. "I like the house and neighborhood and Gramma Vi, too. But there are a lot of grown-up things to figure out before we can make any decisions like that."

"I hope we can." He stared pensively out the window. Then he jumped to his feet. "They're home!" He ran to the back door and flung it open.

Oh, man. Her son was *so* attached to Evan and Lily.

Evan came in on a swirl of wind and snow, holding Lily on his hip. He looked healthy and hearty and happy, and Vanessa's heart almost melted. Lily looked rosy-cheeked, too. "Deh! Deh!" she cried when she saw Declan, holding out her little arms.

Evan got himself and the baby out of their snowy clothes and came farther into the kitchen. "Sure does smell good in here," he said, sniffing appreciatively. "If you need any of that cookie dough tested, I'm your man."

"No, *I'm* your man." Declan grabbed a scrap of sugar cookie dough and stuck it in his mouth.

"No more." Vanessa shook a scolding finger at her son. "That has raw eggs in it. Not good for you."

"Gramma Vi always let me have some," Evan said. When

she mock-glared at him, he amended his statement quickly. "I know it's not good to eat, though. Science has moved along. We'll wait until the cookies are baked."

"Tooky," Lily said.

"She said cookie," Declan said excitedly. "I'm gonna add it to the list." He went to the blackboard next to the stove and wrote "cookie" on the bottom of their growing list.

"What did the doctor say?" Vanessa asked Evan.

"She's going to be fine. She's not even contagious anymore. He gave me an antibiotic. Said she's got an ear infection."

"Ah. Very common. Declan got those all the time. She'll feel better fast if she takes her medicine."

"Can I take her in the living room to play?" Declan asked.

Vanessa glanced at Evan. "Okay with you?"

"Sure."

"Call me when it's time to frost the cookies."

"I will." She watched him back out of the kitchen, making faces and noises to attract Lily into crawling toward him. He was such a sweet kiddo, even if she did say so herself. She could imagine him in a career that had to do with children. Maybe he'd have kids of his own one day.

"I've been thinking," Evan said once Declan and Lily were out of the room. "Do you have a minute to talk?"

She slid the first tray of sugar cookies into the oven and set the timer. "I have ten minutes, to be exact," she said, and sat down.

"I, uh, I have a proposition for you."

She raised an eyebrow. "Oh, really?" she teased.

He didn't take the same tone. "Yes. You've been wonderful with Lily, especially throughout her illness. I really appreciate that."

So this was serious. But something about his attitude gave her an uneasy feeling. "Of course. You know I care for her."

"I'd like to ask you to stay on as her nanny into the foreseeable future."

She tilted her head to one side. This was what Declan wanted.

"I would pay well." He named a salary that was way more than average for a nanny job.

"You don't have to—"

He held up a hand. "I just want to be clear," he said. "This is professional only. I can't go any further with the personal side, not after finding out about Declan's father. What you did would be unacceptable to me in a romantic partner. But I can forgive it for Lily's sake."

Vanessa stared at him, her heart pounding.

It was a good job offer. The salary and living situation were excellent, and she loved caring for Lily. She could help the toddler grow strong, catch up. It was meaningful work.

It was what Declan wanted: to stay right here, in this home he'd become accustomed to, at his same school with his same friends. It would be good for Declan to have Evan as a live-in male role model.

Except…

She felt a weight against her leg. Snickers, leaning against her. She reached down and dug her fingers into his thick, soft fur. When she looked down, she found his warm brown eyes looking up at her with canine intelligence and love.

She looked back at Evan. His smile was slipping a little. It appeared she wasn't responding with delight at his generous offer, at his gracious ability to overlook moral weaknesses in an employee.

If she accepted the offer, she'd always know he'd considered her as a girlfriend and found her lacking. She'd always feel that subtle disgust at her past choices. Choices he hadn't bothered to ask her about. He didn't know the full story, and apparently, he didn't care to. He'd made his judgment.

If she and Declan stayed, how long until that poison wore off on him? How long until he came to share Evan's disdain for his mother and, by extension, for himself?

She was already shaking her head. "No thanks."

"What?" Now the smile was entirely gone. "I thought you liked the work and wanted the job."

She rubbed Snickers's ears, stroked the dog's neck. "I do." She straightened her spine. "But I can't work for a man who carelessly jumps to conclusions about my character without even asking questions about what he's heard."

He frowned. "I thought we'd been over this. The evidence is right there—" he gestured toward the living room "—in Declan. But I'm willing to overlook that. I'm offering you the job."

She blew out a breath. She'd certainly spent plenty of time lamenting her poor choices, but with pastoral counseling and the support of friends like Gramma Vi and Angie, she'd come to have compassion on that lost woman she'd been. "I may have looked for love in all the wrong places," she said, "but I never, ever would have been with a married man. I didn't know, Evan. I didn't know Declan's father was married. Believe me, I cried a river of tears when I found out that all his promises were lies."

His eyebrows drew together. "You're telling me you had no idea he had a wife? How can that be?" His voice had gotten louder.

Vanessa thought of herself as too weak to stand up to anyone. She knew she had to avoid stress at all costs. Well, this situation was stressing her out big-time.

She could still back down, cave in, smile and pretend that

Evan was right about her. The anxiety of having to move and tell Declan and find a new job would be instantly removed if she made that choice.

In the past, she'd have done that. She'd have made the easy choice and told herself it was the right one, that she needed to remain stress-free in order to be a good mother.

But what kind of example was that for Declan? Sometimes, you needed to stand up for yourself, despite how difficult that might be.

She stood with a quick movement that scraped the chair loudly against the floor. Snickers moved away, then came back to her side.

"I thought at one time that I'd tell you the story of me and Declan's father. I thought you were the kind of man who could understand an honest mistake. Who'd have compassion on a young woman who was lost." She looked down at him, still sitting at the table, staring at her with something unreadable in his eyes. "I was wrong. I'll stay through the holidays as we agreed, and then Declan and I will be gone from your life." She turned and strode out of the room, Snickers trotting beside her, past the living room where Declan played with Lily, upstairs where she could keep her bitter tears private from anyone but her faithful dog.

Chapter Fifteen

Evan sat in the kitchen until the smell of something burning brought him to his feet. By the time he realized what was happening and grabbed a pot holder, the cookies Vanessa had made were burned into a dozen crisp, black Christmas trees and Santas and wreaths.

He didn't want to tell Declan that he'd upset his mom and so the cookie baking was a no-go. He didn't quite understand where he'd gone wrong with Vanessa.

Most of all, he was worried about Lily. She'd been thriving here with Vanessa as her nanny and Declan as a stand-in big brother. Now, Vanessa was saying she and Declan would be out of here after the holidays.

He paced the kitchen, wondering what to do, worrying that he'd gone about the conversation all wrong, angry that Vanessa had taken his job offer the wrong way and gotten insulted.

He mostly ignored the ache in his heart. That, he could deal with later.

"Evan! Mom! Look!" It was Declan, calling from the living room.

Evan went in.

"Watch! I got her to walk!" Declan set Lily on her feet, leaning her back against the couch for support. Then he picked up one of her dolls and backed a couple of yards away. "Come on," he said, waving the toy.

Lily reached out her hands. "Deh! Deh!"

"Come on, you can do it!" Declan held out his hands to where they almost touched Lily's.

She took one step, then another, before she started to teeter. Declan grabbed her hands, eased her down to a sitting position and put the toy in her arms. "Did you see?"

"I did," Evan said through a tight throat. "You did great, both of you." He knelt on the floor and tugged Lily into his arms. Then he held out a hand to Declan. The boy leaned in, and they had an awkward triple hug.

"Where's Mom? I want to show her. What's that smell?"

"She, uh, wasn't feeling well and she went upstairs. I'm afraid I let the cookies burn."

"Aw, man." Declan's face fell.

Evan felt bad about the cookies, but not as bad as he felt about Vanessa. And he was terribly worried what would happen if Lily lost another caregiver so soon after being abandoned by her mother.

He needed to talk to someone. But who? He didn't have close friends in town. His grandmother was one possibility, but he felt somehow ashamed to talk to her. Plus, the Christmas luncheon at the rehab center was today. Gramma had gotten deeply involved in the place's social life and would want to attend. Was probably helping to organize activities for it.

And then it dawned on him. Luke and Angie had come to their aid when Lily had gotten sick. Maybe they could help him figure out how to get Vanessa to stay on as Lily's nanny.

A couple of texts, and it was agreed: he'd bring Lily over for a playdate with little Charlotte, and the grown-ups could talk. They suggested bringing Declan, too, since their older kids were home.

"Want to go with me to see your uncle and Angie and the kids?" Evan asked.

Declan thought about it, then shook his head. "I'd better stay home with Mom, if she's not feeling well."

What a great kid Declan was. Evan's determination to find a way to make Vanessa change her mind increased. He'd figure out how with Luke's and Angie's help, and he'd get this fixed before Christmas.

An hour later, he was seated at Angie and Luke's kitchen table. Lily and Charlotte played on a climbing structure in the corner of the kitchen.

He'd come here for help and support, but so far, that wasn't how the conversation was going.

"You told her *what*?" Angie sounded disbelieving.

"I offered her the nanny job, with a big pay raise and live-in privileges, not just for her, but for Declan. She turned me down cold."

"No, before that. The part where you told her she was good enough to be a nanny, but not good enough to be a girlfriend," Angie said bluntly.

Luke had been quietly stewing throughout the conversation, his face getting redder and redder. Now he stood, and for a minute Evan was pretty sure the guy was going to deck him. He glared down at Evan, fists clenched. "My sister's good enough for anyone. Way too good for the likes of you."

Angie put a hand on Luke's arm. "Why don't you go check on Vanessa and Declan?" she suggested. "I'll take care of this." She waved a hand to indicate the house, the kids and Evan.

Luke's eyes narrowed. His fists were still clenched.

"Luke. Go. I've got this." Angie gave her husband a gentle nudge toward the door.

"All right." Luke turned, took a step and then turned back. His face was hard, unsmiling. "Just remember, Vanessa isn't alone in the world. She's got me, and I won't let anyone treat her poorly."

"Understood."

"She's a good mother, and a good friend, and a good sister."

"I believe you."

Luke glared at him for another moment and then stomped out of the room, his work boots loud against the hardwood floor.

Evan and Angie both waited until they heard Luke's truck start up and drive away, spitting gravel.

"It's a good thing he left," Angie said. "He's protective of Vanessa, and for good reason." She walked over to the coffeepot.

"Of course. He's her brother." Evan frowned. "What I don't get is why I feel like the bad guy, when it was Vanessa who did something wrong."

Angie paused in the act of pouring coffee. "What did she do wrong?"

"She—she went with a married man," Evan sputtered. "*Your* husband, and I assume that wasn't okay with you." He felt his face heating. He hadn't intended to get this granular with poor Angie, who was a victim of both her late husband and Vanessa.

"Wow." Angie plunked his coffee cup on the table and shoved sugar and creamer in his direction. "I can totally see why she doesn't want to work for you."

Evan lifted his hands, palms up. "Am I wrong here? Is adultery okay?"

She rolled her eyes. "Of course not. But you're way oversimplifying. Vanessa didn't know Oscar was married when she got together with him."

"You believe that?"

Lily made a fussy sound, and Evan went over to check on her. Charlotte had snatched her doll away and was using it to pound the floor. "Hey, hey," he said, putting out a hand to stop the banging. "Let's be gentle with the babies."

Both little girls looked at him blankly.

He saw another half-naked baby doll lying on the floor and picked it up. He cradled it in his arms as if it were a real baby. "Aww, such a nice baby," he crooned, rocking it back and forth.

Charlotte let Lily's doll drop to the floor. "Mine!" she said, reaching for the one Evan was holding.

He gave it to her, handed Lily her own doll and backed up to the kitchen table. The little girls both cradled their baby dolls as he had done.

"Nice," Angie said, smiling briefly. Then she propped her elbows on the table and leaned toward him. "Vanessa *didn't* know Oscar was married. She came to me and explained, after everything came to a head. It took time, and talk, but I forgave her. More than that, I've come to love her like a sister. She's a good person who's had a very hard row to hoe, and she's getting better and better." She frowned. "I just hope you haven't set her back."

This was going off track. Evan didn't want to follow in Angie's soft, forgiving footsteps; he wanted to focus on facts. "Whatever the situation, she had a child to a married man, out of wedlock."

"Take away the 'married' part, since she didn't know Oscar was married. So that leaves the fact that she had a child out of wedlock. Which isn't ideal, but it's also very common. Would you reject any woman with that background?"

Reject was a hard word. He tried to explain. "I'm not judging, it's just, that's not what I want for myself. I want what you and Luke have." He waved a hand around. "The happy home, the kids, the trust between you."

"Uh-huh." Angie stirred creamer into her coffee, then tilted her head to one side. "Did you know I used to be an exotic dancer?"

"What?" Evan had to stop himself from backing away. "But you're so..."

"Normal? Nice?" Angie didn't give him time to respond. "Evan, all that normal is just on the surface. Scratch it, and you'll find a whole lot of flaws inside almost everyone." She studied him shrewdly. "You included, although your flaws may run more in the line of judgment and legalism. Kind of like the Pharisees, you know?"

Evan blinked. The little girls babbled now, half in real words, half in nonsense syllables. His coffee, dark and rich, sat before him, untasted. Winter sun slanted through the windows.

"That's why we need Christ," Angie went on. "Because we're *all* a mess. Vanessa and Luke grew up without a mom. They went into foster care after their dad died by suicide. Luke got away and shaped up in the military, but Vanessa made different choices. Not ones she's proud of, any more than I'm proud of my past, but with God's help, she's healing." She frowned. "She tends to be hard on herself. Doesn't think she's strong, but you know what? She's one of the strongest people I know."

Evan let his face drop into his hands. When he looked up, Angie was watching him. "I know you think you have a nanny problem," she said. "I'd call it more of an outlook problem. Thinking you're better than other people. Feeling free to judge. That's not Christian, Evan. I'm sure you have your reasons for it, and maybe you ought to dig for them at some point. But until you get over yourself, no way would I even try to talk Vanessa into continuing to work for you."

Evan left a few minutes later, reeling. Was he really a Pharisee? Did he think he was better than others? Had he judged Vanessa too harshly? Did he have a right to judge her at all?

And if Angie was right, and Evan was wrong, what did it mean for Lily, who needed way more than just him to grow up? Who needed a good role model?

What did it mean for Evan, who was starting to realize he'd never really understood love and forgiveness?

On Christmas Eve, Vanessa found herself alone in the church hall, preparing cookie trays and hot chocolate urns for after services. Alone except for Snickers, who lay quietly at the side of the big room, head on paws, watching her every move.

Declan was with another boy, both of them helping with candle lighting and ushering people into the sanctuary. Evan had Lily, not that Vanessa had spoken with him; they'd arranged for her care by text, with Evan doing the bulk of it since his misguided job offer on Monday night.

Vanessa was still upset about what had happened. A little bit angry, but mostly sad for what could have been. She and Evan had started to build something, and it was hard to see that structure come crashing to the ground.

Everything that had happened this week would have, at one time, thrown her into a tailspin. Stress had been her middle name in the past few days, and yet she was handling it with lots of prayer and of course, with Snickers's help.

Behind her sadness, there was a small flame of pride that was growing each day. After all, she'd done the near impossible. In the last forty-eight hours, she'd found herself and Declan a new place to live, in the same school district. It had involved calling everyone she knew, and combing the internet and the ads, and visiting the few possible places. In the end, she'd done it. She'd explained why it was necessary, too, to Declan: she'd told him that the grown-ups had made a decision that it was best for them to move out. That they could still see Gramma—the new place wasn't far away from where they lived now—and his friends. In fact, their new home was a carriage house behind his friend Caleb's place. It was adorable, and Vanessa couldn't wait to get started decorating it.

It was affordable, too. The money she was making as Lily's nanny had helped, but the real coup was that she had leads on two different jobs in childcare. One of them was a head teacher role and would require her to be working on an education degree. That was a little scary. But she was starting to think she might be strong enough to do something scary. She already *was* doing scary things and surviving them.

Despite being sad about Evan's cruel attitude, she felt stronger. The past week had made her understand that strength came from doing things, from facing and working through problems rather than avoiding them.

"There you are!" Gramma Vi came into the hall, decked out in a bright red pantsuit. Even her cane had tinsel wrapped around it.

Vanessa hurried over and they hugged. "I'm looking forward to a few days at home with you and Declan," Gramma said. "And Evan, of course. He dropped me off and will be in once he's found a place to park."

The thought of those days at home with Evan, Declan,

Lily and Gramma made Vanessa's heart pound faster, and not in a good way. But she'd get through it.

Snickers came over, clearly glad to see Gramma Vi, his tail wagging, so Vanessa released him for Gramma to pet. After they'd chatted for a few minutes and greeted other church members, Vanessa pulled Gramma Vi aside. "I wanted to let you know that I'm thinking Declan and I will move out. But if you need me as a caregiver when you come home, we'll work out a way for that to happen. I'm still here for you."

Gramma looked at her sharply. "So you and my grandson aren't..." She trailed off.

"No," Vanessa said. "But I'm here for you."

The older woman studied her. "I'm glad to see you're okay. Are you eating right?"

Vanessa blinked. "Yes. Yes, I am." In the midst of all that had happened in the past few days, she'd never starved herself nor wanted to.

They were standing near the church entrance. Evan came in, his hair covered with a light dusting of snow, Lily on his hip. Vanessa's heart tugged toward him. He was so handsome, and in many ways, such a good person.

"Sit with us?" Gramma offered, looking at Vanessa.

"No, not now." She reached down and put a hand on Snickers's head. "I'll see you afterward."

The service was rich in scriptures that told the Christmas story. Vanessa inhaled the fragrance of evergreen branches and candles and listened to the sound of people's voices raised as they enthusiastically sang favorite Christmas hymns.

As never before, Vanessa was struck by the strength Mary had shown. She'd borne a child out of wedlock, facing shame from others, and yet she'd done as God had commanded her.

Vanessa looked over at Gramma Vi. She sat listening to scripture, her wrinkled face lit by the candle at the end of her pew, her smile peaceful. She was a strong woman, too, who'd taken in her grandson and raised him, who was now facing physical challenges with courage and grace.

After the service, Angie came and hugged her and wished her a Merry Christmas. They'd talked several times during the past couple of days, so Angie knew the basics of what was going on.

Vanessa reached down and rubbed Snickers's shaggy head. "Question for you," she asked Angie. "About Snickers. If I'm ever, you know, okay, if I'm making mostly healthy choices for a while, do you think I have to give him up?"

"No, of course not," Angie said. "If you feel that you don't need him to be a full-time service dog, he can still be your pet. Maybe he could even do some therapy work, since he's so well-trained."

An idea pressed into Vanessa's mind. Maybe a therapy dog would be helpful to women struggling with anorexia, at a facility or at group meetings.

Declan came over to her. "Ready to go? I'm hungry!"

"Of course." She waved to Gramma. "We'll see you back at the house, late tonight or else tomorrow."

She ignored Evan, or at least, she didn't speak to him. But she couldn't help feeling sad at the sight of him. They could have been good together, if things had been different.

If not for Declan and Gramma, she would have definitely spared herself the pain of spending more time in the same house with Evan. But she was strong enough to do it now. She was sure of it.

Chapter Sixteen

After Christmas Eve services, Evan drove Gramma Vi back home. It was a delight to see how happy she was to be spending Christmas there. He'd already laid a fire, so he lit it and settled her beside it while he brought in her things.

Lily was sleepy, so he lay her down in the playpen for now. She'd go to bed soon, but Gramma loved being near her, and it seemed right to all be together on Christmas Eve.

Except they weren't all together. Vanessa and Declan had gone over to Luke and Angie's place for a late Christmas Eve dinner and gift opening. They wouldn't be home until close to midnight, Vanessa had told him in one of her chilly texts.

Soon he and Gramma were settled in wing chairs on either side of the fireplace, sipping hot chocolate. The fire put out a welcome warmth he could feel on his legs. The tall tree glittered with multicolored lights and Gramma's vintage ornaments, and there were a few gifts beneath it. He'd gotten things for Gramma and Declan and Lily, and Gramma had brought gifts for everyone. There were a few gifts from Vanessa, but he hadn't looked to see who the recipients were. Certainly not him.

"What's on your mind?" Gramma asked.

He met her shrewd gaze. "That obvious, huh?"

"I know you pretty well, after all these years." She sipped

her hot chocolate and carefully put her cup down. "You seem kind of...pensive."

"I do want to ask you something. Do you think I'm judgmental?"

She tilted her head to one side. "Interesting question. Yes, you definitely are, but why do you ask?"

Ouch. He hadn't expected Gramma to answer "yes" quite so quickly. "I learned something about Vanessa that threw me for a loop. I let her know how I felt, and I guess...that may have been a bad idea."

"Did you learn about Declan's father?"

"Yes." He leaned forward and poked at the fire, sending up a fountain of sparks. "I didn't know if you were aware."

"Mrs. Fenstermaker mentioned it when she came to visit. It lined up with the little Vanessa had mentioned or implied."

"So you see why I...why it changed my view of her."

"I do." She settled more comfortably into her chair. "You remember the part of your childhood where your mom cheated and left the family."

He'd never heard Gramma put it so baldly before. *He* did, in his own mind, but he'd never heard Gramma say it like that. "I've never forgiven her for that," he said. "Not that I've had the opportunity." They'd tried to find her a couple of times during his teenage years, but she seemed to have disappeared from the face of the earth. Most likely, they'd figured out, she had died.

She leaned forward. "You don't remember much before that happened, do you?"

He shook his head. "I was, what, eight when she left? Nine when I came to live here full-time?"

"Right." She sighed. "Before that, there was so much fighting in your home. It was a very violent situation, and I'm sure you've blocked out most of it."

He had dim memories of shouting and slamming doors, but not much else. "I guess I did."

She nodded. "Even if you don't remember it consciously, that kind of thing has a big effect on a child's nervous system. You, like most kids, thought that if you were good enough, you could save your parents from each other. You were the most tense child I've ever met when you came to me. Walking on eggshells. It took a lot of time and love before you could relax, even a little."

"I don't really remember that."

"You wouldn't. Like I said, kids block it out. But one of the consequences, from the reading I've done, is that you judge yourself harshly. It's a preventative thing. If you can be watchful enough to find and fix your own flaws, then the bad things won't happen. Only, of course, that's a mistaken view. Your mom still left, and then your dad."

Lily let out a little cry in her sleep, and he walked over and put her stuffed toy back into her arms. Her face relaxed again.

Gramma wasn't finished. "You judge others harshly because you think you'll be able to control them. That part comes later. When you came to me, you weren't judging your parents, you were just heartbroken. I think getting angry at them was probably a healthy defense mechanism."

"But shouldn't I be angry that Mom cheated?"

She lifted her hands, palms up. "It was wrong. But it wasn't even the main thing that affected you. That damage was done long before, with the screaming and the throwing things and the neglect of you while all that was happening."

"Why is this the first time I'm hearing about it?" he asked.

"I made the decision not to tell you. You'd blocked a lot, and you already had so much anger toward your parents. I didn't want to add to that. Whether I was right or wrong, I don't know." She rubbed the cast on her wrist. "Do you remember anything from your early years, now that we're talking about it? Christmas was especially bad, like in a lot of homes with domestic violence."

He closed his eyes and tried to call up his earliest memories. "Did someone knock over a Christmas tree?"

"Yes. You cut yourself badly trying to clean up all the broken glass ornaments. When I arrived on Christmas Day, your hands were a wreck. You were only six, but you'd found dish towels to wrap them in so the blood wouldn't make a mess. You were sitting on the couch waiting for me."

Her words evoked a physical memory. He remembered that he'd been sweating, his heart pounding with fear. She'd come in the door, taken one look at the scene, and pulled him into her arms.

He'd loved her so much, then.

All of a sudden his throat was so tight he couldn't speak. He cleared it, then took a gulp of hot chocolate, then knelt in front of the fire to poke at it, trying to regain control of his emotions.

"It's a lot," Gramma said, reaching forward to rub his back the way she'd done when he was much younger. "Take some time to process it and pray about it. Pray for healing."

"*Can* I be healed?" he asked her.

"Oh, Evan." She leaned forward farther and gave him a full-on hug, and he hugged her back, kneeling beside her chair.

"You're already an amazing man," she said. "Look how successful you are. You have a big career, and yet when Lily needed you, you dropped everything to care for her. You're managing really well."

Evan couldn't agree.

"What you haven't managed well, you may be able to repair. And pertinent to that, Vanessa told me she's considering moving out."

He'd known it was likely, and yet hearing it was a blow.

"You've heaped some things on her that may actually come from your own past," Gramma said. "But it's Christmastime, and special things happen at Christmastime. I wonder if you can fix it?" She smiled at him, her eyes twinkling.

He hugged her. "I know one thing. You've been a wonderful support to me all these years. Thank you for that."

"I've loved every minute of being your gramma," she said.

He helped her to the bedroom he'd been using. Then he carried Lily into the room he'd now be sharing with her and tucked her in. He sank into the rocking chair and kept thinking about all of it.

His ideas about the world were just that: ideas. They'd come from places buried deep inside himself. Now, he faced the problem of trying to undo the damage he'd done.

He thought of Vanessa, who'd had her own difficult upbringing, according to Angie. He thought of Declan, who'd been raised better.

He looked at Lily through the slats of her crib. She looked so peaceful, so innocent. She *was* an innocent. And he was responsible for raising her right.

If he didn't fix some of the holes in himself, he'd pass along his flawed ideas to her. And what could be worse for a little girl than sensing that her father had a grudge against the entire female gender?

The grudge was wrong. There were wonderful, strong women surrounding him. Chief of all was Gramma, who'd given up a peaceful retirement to raise a troubled little boy and raise him well. But there were also women like Angie and Vanessa. Neither had had things easy, but they'd become women of power who could be great role models to Lily.

Unless he'd pushed them away by his own foolish words and ignorant attitudes. When he thought of what he'd said to Vanessa—that she wasn't worthy to be his girlfriend—he cringed, appalled at himself.

He leaned his head back against the rocking chair, looking heavenward. It was going to take a lot of help from God to fix this.

It was one of the most beautiful Christmas mornings Vanessa had ever experienced. They'd left the living room ankle-deep in wrapping paper and had come into the kitchen for breakfast. Sun streamed through the windows, brighter for the dusting of snow on the ground and in the trees. They'd worked together to cook breakfast, and they'd all eaten heartily. The fragrance of cinnamon rolls, bacon and coffee still hung in the air, and everyone, even Evan and Declan, had pushed away from the table.

Vanessa's stomach was full and her heart was, too. Except for the little piece of it that ached because she and Evan were still awkward and at odds.

She knew she had to move out and move on, but it wasn't going to be easy. In many ways, what she'd always wanted was right here in this room.

Lily squirmed in her booster chair, and Vanessa lifted her out of it and held her in her lap, bouncing her gently, feeling an ache deep in her chest. Such a sweet baby. Vanessa would really, really miss her.

"I'm gonna play with my new drone," Declan said. It was Evan's gift to him, way too expensive, but Vanessa wasn't going to object. "And my Lego set," he added quickly, looking at her.

"You can enjoy them both," she reassured him. Such a kind boy. He didn't want her to feel bad about her moderately priced gift. "Go. Have fun."

"I'm going to nap," Gramma said. "On the couch, so

I can watch the tree lights sparkle. And watch my great-granddaughter."

"She'll probably take a nap, too," Evan said. "This was a lot of excitement today, and she's still recovering from being sick."

Vanessa smiled. Evan sounded more like an experienced parent every day.

After Declan, Lily and Gramma were settled in the living room, Vanessa started cleaning up from breakfast. Evan came in and quietly started helping her.

"You don't have to," she said. "Go relax with the others."

"I want to help. And... I wondered if you'd take a walk with me once we're done. I would like to talk with you."

More pain? She wasn't up for that. "It depends. Are you going to be mean to me?"

He winced. "No. Give me half an hour, and then if you don't like what I have to say, we'll be done."

She'd figured they would need to talk at some point. May as well do it now, on a beautiful Christmas morning. "I could use the exercise to walk off those cinnamon rolls," she said. "Let me get Snickers ready."

She snapped her fingers for the dog and put on the red designer collar Evan had gotten him, then snapped on his service vest and leash.

Declan had gone upstairs to call his friend Caleb, eager to talk about the drones they'd both received as gifts. She looked in on him and he waved, but clearly didn't need his mom interrupting him. Then she went into the living room. Both Gramma and Lily were asleep.

She was delaying. She put a hand on the new devotional Bible Gramma had gotten her and thought, *I can handle this. I know my priorities: God and Declan.*

Moments later, Vanessa and Evan were walking through town toward the bay, their breath making clouds in the cold air.

They weren't the only ones out taking advantage of the glorious sunshine. Several family groups greeted them with waves and "Merry Christmas" greetings.

Evan wore jeans, a brown leather jacket and a scarf Gramma had knitted for him, bright red. No hat, and now he scraped his fingers through his hair. "First off, I want to apologize. I was way out of line in what I said about you, that you weren't moral enough to have a personal relationship with. There was no excuse for that, and I'm ashamed of myself."

Wow. She wasn't sure what she'd been expecting, but it wasn't that.

"I don't expect you to forgive me," he said, "but I want you to know that I realize how wrong I was and I'm sorry."

She glanced over at him. He looked miserable, staring down at his boots as he walked, slowly.

She waited until he met her eyes, then spoke. "I've tried to teach Declan to apologize well," she said. "Now I see I could have outsourced that job to you."

"I'm sincere," he said quickly. "It's not just a...technique."

"No, I can see that." She wondered whether to accept his apology or to make him suffer. But it was Christmas, and she was feeling benevolent. And strong. "I accept your apology," she said.

Another mother from Declan's class passed them, speed-walking with an older woman who must be her mother. They all waved.

They reached the bay, which stretched out endlessly, sparkling in the sunshine. They turned and walked along the boardwalk.

"I'm starting to realize," Evan said, "how negative and judgmental I can be. What happened with you really crystalized that, and Gramma helped me understand where it's coming from."

She didn't want him piling *all* the guilt on his own head. "It could be from how badly I treated you when I ended things before. I never apologized for that, but I am sorry. I thought you were too good for me, but I had a really bad way of showing it and I hurt you. I'm sorry for that."

"Thank you and I accept," he said. "But it's me who wasn't good enough for you. I hadn't worked through anything in my childhood. I still haven't, really. But I need to, for Lily's sake and for..." He broke off. A seagull flew overhead, with a loud cry. The slightly salty smell of the bay rose around them.

She looked at him out of the corner of her eye. He was struggling so earnestly that she wanted to reach out and pull him into her arms.

He looked over and met her eyes. "In my limited way, I cared for you deeply back then. And I care even more deeply now."

Her heart rate picked up its pace. She so, so wanted to believe him. But could she? Should she?

"I can't expect you to want to date me or anything, not after what a jerk I was, but I want you to know that I'm going to work toward being a man worthy of dating you."

"That's a turnaround." He'd thought she was unworthy of him just a few days ago.

"I needed to be turned around," he said. "I had it all backward. You're the one who's strong, and kind, and caring. I love that about you. The way you are with Gramma, and especially with Lily... You've made such a huge difference to her already."

Emotions welled up inside her. To push them away, she tried to joke. "Is this all a ploy to get me to be Lily's nanny longer term?"

"No!" He stopped and turned to face her. "But, would you consider that, while I work on myself in hopes of one day being more to you than an employer?"

She gestured to a bench, and they sat down. "I'd like to stay connected to Lily and to Gramma, too. But, Evan, I'm going to move out. I've found another place for me and Declan."

"Gramma told me. It makes me sad, but I understand."

He did look sad. And maybe it was wrong of her, even weak, but she didn't want to leave him that way. "You know," she said, "even though I did get upset with what you said, I still think you're the best man I've ever cared for."

He looked at her quickly. "Do you still care, a little?"

She studied him, biting her lip. To say yes—which was the truth—might mean a loss of power.

But the praying she'd done came back in a reassuring wave of grace. "I do. I still feel drawn toward you. You've been wonderful toward Lily, and you're good for Declan. And...you're kind of cute."

"Cute?" He raised an eyebrow.

"Uh-huh." She squeezed his arm. "And manly and smart and a real gentleman."

Her words had the effect of lifting his face, taking away some of its careworn expression. "That gives me courage to say that... I want you, Vanessa."

She raised an eyebrow. "Meaning..."

"I may as well say it. I already know I want to marry you."

She sucked in a breath, her heart leaping.

"Not that you'll agree to even date me, but for me, you've always been in my heart since that first night I took you home to Gramma with a broken wrist. Now, seeing what you're like as a mature woman, I know it more. You're the woman I want to spend the rest of my life with."

Tears filled Vanessa's eyes. Before, she'd thought a man like Evan was too good and perfect for her. Now, she realized he was flawed and human, like anyone else. But she still thought he was perfect for her. And now, finally, she felt worthy of being with someone like Evan. "We'd have to take it slow," she said. "There's Declan to consider, and Lily. And we both need to keep working on ourselves."

"Agreed, but...can we go out on a few dates, too?"

She smiled at him. "Well...maybe."

He took her hand, pulled it to his lips and kissed it. Then he looked into her eyes. "And what about being Lily's nanny? It's up to you, and whatever you decide, it doesn't change how I feel about you."

"I have a better idea." She told him about the head teacher job offer she'd received. "Lily's so social, and she would advance faster being with other kids. It's a small day care, pretty expensive, but she'd be with me."

He studied her. "I think...that might work."

"And then I wouldn't be your employee."

"True." Light began to dawn in his eyes.

"So we *could* go out on dates if we wanted to, without it being weird."

"I'm loving this idea. I'm loving..." He stopped. "I don't want to overstep, but I'm happier than I ever thought I could be."

She leaned toward him just as he leaned toward her. They met halfway, and the kiss they shared was as tender and sweet and promising as Christmas morning.

She was happier than she'd ever been, too. And this was just the beginning.

Epilogue

Winter flew by in a haze of learning a new job and fixing up a new rental cottage, but Vanessa could do it all because she had Evan to help and support her efforts. He listened to her description of challenges at work, but didn't give advice unless she asked him to. He moved furniture around, sometimes over and over, until she had the carriage house just the way she wanted it. If he spent a little too much time making sure each picture he hung for her was perfectly level, she laughed and loved him for it.

She'd stayed in therapy but had cut down the frequency to once a month. Snickers was still at her side at home and during her free time. She didn't take him to work with her most days, though. Didn't need to. She could manage without him. Now, she and Declan were training him to be a therapy dog with Angie's help.

Evan had worked out a way to stay in Chesapeake Corners and keep his job, working remotely most of the time. Once a month, he had to go into the city to work, but for the most part, he lived in Gramma's place with her and a visiting caregiver. That wouldn't last forever, though. Gramma was thinking of moving into an assisted-living community, because she'd realized she loved the social aspect of it. She was more and more mobile and active, one of those fortunate seniors who recovered completely from broken bones.

Today, at the start of May, they were planting a garden at Gramma's place. Gramma sat in the warm sunshine, looking on and making suggestions, sometimes leaning over to pull an early weed. Snickers sniffed around the edge of the yard, looking for squirrels to chase.

Lily toddled around, talking to Declan and Gramma in intelligible three-word sentences. Going to the day care had worked wonders for her development, and she was on track to stop her early intervention services soon.

"Dig here, Mom!" Declan beckoned to a corner of the garden.

"Why?"

"Just dig," he said. "I think, um, the radishes should go here."

"He's right," Gramma said. "You have to dig and till the soil first to grow radishes. Now, I believe I'll go inside, if Declan will help me."

Declan ran over and helped her up, then beckoned to Lily, who took his other hand. The trio made their way toward the house.

Evan stood in the corner of the garden that Declan and Gramma had indicated. "Are you going to dig?" He was smiling, so warm, back to his confident self, only it wasn't so brittle this time. He was more relaxed than she'd ever seen him, and it was a really, really good look. He continued to work on himself, with weekly counseling sessions with the pastor, and he was resolving his issues from his past.

She looked at the corner of the garden, then at Evan. She shrugged and hugged him. "Whatever you say." She dug, and her small spade hit something. A stone? No, a plastic box. What in the world?

She looked up at Evan. He was smiling. He wore jeans and a T-shirt, his face flushed from his work in the sun. She felt the same thrill she always did, being close to him.

Carefully, she dug it out.

"Open it," Evan said. His voice sounded...odd.

Something was going on. She opened the plastic container and caught her breath. Inside was a small velvet box. She looked up at Evan. "Is this..." She trailed off.

He knelt in front of her. "Open it. And then tell me if you'll marry me."

She gasped, looking from his handsome face to the box and back again. The idea of being joined with this man forever filled her with joy. She set down the box and grasped his hands. "I don't even need to open it. I will."

"Yes!" He pulled her into his arms.

Their embrace was short-lived, because Declan, who must have sneaked out the back door, was shouting. "She said yes! Open the box, Mom! I caught it all on camera!"

So she did. She slipped the tasteful square-cut diamond on her finger. Of course it fit perfectly. Evan would have found a way to make sure of that. It was the kind of man he was.

"I love it," she said, holding it up to reflect the spring sunshine. She looked up at the man who would, thanks to God's saving grace, become her husband. "And I love you." She held out her arms, and Evan embraced her again. He beckoned to Declan, and even though Declan considered himself too old for hugs, he joined in. Snickers ran around them in circles, barking, and that brought Gramma and Lily out to join the group hug.

Surrounded by the people she loved most, Vanessa knew that healing was possible and grace was real. She inhaled the rich air of springtime and breathed a wordless prayer of thanks.

* * * * *

If you enjoyed this K-9 Companions story by Lee Tobin McClain, pick up her other K-9 Companions books set in Chesapeake Corners:

Holding Onto Secrets
Her Surprise Neighbor

Available now from Love Inspired!

And don't miss another fantastic K-9 Companions book from Love Inspired, An Alaskan Christmas Prayer *by Belle Calhoune, on sale December 2025!*

Dear Reader,

Thank you for joining me for another K-9 Companions story set in Chesapeake Corners, Maryland.

I always gravitated toward science and math nerds, even though I'm the literary type. Like my real-life nerd friends, my hero Evan is a little awkward and very smart, and he has a huge heart. He's steadfastly loyal to his grandmother. He assumes full care of his daughter without a second thought. And he longs to make things work with Vanessa, even though it takes him a little while to realize that and figure out how to do it!

I did a lot of research on anorexia, but Vanessa came to life because of experiences I had with an extended family member who struggled with an eating disorder. She was brilliant and fun and heartbreakingly beautiful, but she wasn't able to recover during the time that I knew her. Through Vanessa, I was able to rewrite her story, giving her love and faith and a happy ending.

On a lighter note, I hope you enjoyed meeting Declan, Lily, Gramma Vi and Snickers. I had so much fun creating a wonderful Christmas season for them.

It's you, my readers, who allow me to continue crafting characters and stories to share. Thank you for that! I would love to have you visit my website and join my newsletter, where you'll find news, freebies and giveaways.

Wishing you Christmas joy,
Lee